Her voice
turned accusi

"You picked me out of the crowd at the reception not because you thought I was pretty—" Caitlin's tone mocked him and herself for believing him "—but because I'm Jim Stewart's widow."

"That's not true," Lee said quietly moving closer to her. Suddenly Caitlin was overwhelmingly aware of his broad shoulders and how small the car was.

"My husband would never be involved in anything illegal," she angrily retorted.

"Forget your late husband," Lee growled. "Let's talk about *this*." He reached out and put one hand over hers. The current that ran between them was as tangible as an electric shock.

Caitlin snatched her hand away as if she'd been burned. She didn't want to respond to Lee Michaels. "I can't even understand why I'm here in this car with you—"

He closed the space between them. "Can't you?"

Kelly Street always enjoyed the "romancy parts" of novels best, so when she fulfilled her ambition to become a writer she chose, of course, to write a Temptation romance. Happily married to a dean, Kelly is very familiar with university life and used her experiences at several different campuses to create Tall Pines University. The football portions of the book, however, involved some "homework"—she and her husband watched a lot of Forty-Niner games. The Streets make their home in Spokane, Washington, with their son and daughter and their favorite feline, Meringue.

Only Human
KELLY STREET

Harlequin Books

TORONTO • NEW YORK • LONDON
AMSTERDAM • PARIS • SYDNEY • HAMBURG
STOCKHOLM • ATHENS • TOKYO • MILAN

For the men in my life,
Jerry and Christopher

Published April 1990

ISBN 0-373-25394-X

1

"DON'T DRINK THAT!"

Caitlin Stewart paused with the plastic glass only an inch from her nose. She looked up—way up—at blue eyes, vivid in a darkly tanned and completely unfamiliar male face. Astonished, she said, "I beg your pardon?"

The stranger grinned, revealing white teeth. "I said, don't drink that. It's terrible."

Caitlin pulled her gaze from the smiling eyes and looked into her glass. It was filled almost to the brim with the very bad white wine traditionally served at faculty parties. "How can you say so? I happen to know this wine came all the way from Idaho."

The man's bass chuckle was so deep it sounded intimate, even though they were being jostled by a crowd of professors anxious to get to the bar.

He said, "Well, it could be the way you crinkle your nose when you gird yourself to try it. Or the expression on your face after each taste. Or," he added as he firmly removed the glass from her grasp, "it could be because a few minutes ago I had the misfortune to drink some myself and dumped the rest into the aspidistra over there."

"That's not an aspidistra, it's a rhododendron, and you probably killed it."

The frank enjoyment with which he was regarding her brought burning color into her cheeks. Three years of widowhood had provided her with ample opportunity to develop her technique for freezing too-friendly males in their tracks, but this one was succeeding in unsettling her.

Of course Caitlin had arrived at the reception feeling harassed and uncomfortable, which was why she had so much wine in her glass. Anything to do with football automatically brought back memories of her short marriage, of a vibrant and vital Jim coaching, throwing himself into those everlasting practice games like one of the college players less than half his age.

A party celebrating the new season of football at Tall Pines University, a season without the late Coach Jim Stewart, was bad enough. Even worse was the reason behind the bravado that had inspired this wretched affair; TPU wanted the world to know it wasn't concerned about the investigation the college athletic conference was making into its recruiting policies. She wondered if the university's officers imagined they were fooling anyone. The thought of scandal touching the team—Jim's team—put a hollow feeling in the pit of Caitlin's stomach.

"May I have my drink back, please?" she said. "I think I need it."

The stranger raised very dark brows. He didn't look much older than Caitlin—at the most, he might be thirty, she thought—but something confident about the set of his broad shoulders, the tilt of that decided chin, argued that he didn't often have much trouble chatting up women, even in a venue as unlikely as this one.

He asked kindly, "A medicinal draught?"

A reluctant smile tugged at her lips. "More or less. I really didn't want to come here today."

"No?" He glanced around. TPU's largest reception hall was ornately Victorian, with gold foil on the ceiling and oak wainscoting on the walls. Long graceful windows admitted late-afternoon sunlight that lit Caitlin's casual swirl of red hair to the copper of new pennies. "It looks like a nice enough joint. Don't you like academic clambakes?"

"Normally I can stand them. I work for the university, in the library." Nervousness was making Caitlin vocal. "Faculty parties are sort of an occupational hazard," she said with a grimace which sat oddly on her delicate features.

"A librarian? You certainly don't fit the popular conception," he told her, contemplating her heart-shaped face and the trim, high-breasted figure that didn't quite attain sexlessness in a severe gray suit.

"The popular misconception," she corrected briskly. "For your information, librarians come in all sizes and shapes and both sexes. *You* could be one."

Actually, she admitted to herself, he didn't look like any male librarian she'd ever met.

He was tall, especially compared to her five feet two inches. She wondered if he found her short. His black curls, trimmed short so they hugged his head, topped her maximum height in heels by a foot. Maybe from his height everybody looked short, she thought hopefully, and didn't even realize she was forgetting that she'd sworn off noticing men's looks a long time ago. The tweedy jacket and conservative shirt and tie he was wearing were appropriate to the surroundings but they didn't cover one of the burgeoning paunches or hollow chests that abounded in this gathering.

In fact, his athletic body and aquiline features, lit by those incredible blue eyes, were almost a shock every time she glanced at them. How could any man be so good-looking?

He chuckled again. "Nothing so respectable. But are you sure you're old enough to have gone to graduate school? You look about nineteen."

"Twenty-six, thank you," Caitlin said. "A very staid and unfortunately very sober twenty-six." Her pointed stare at the glass he still held in one brown and competent-looking hand underlined her remark.

"I'll tell you what. Why don't you let me buy you a decent drink?"

Caitlin said blankly, "You mean go somewhere off campus?"

His brows drew together quizzically. "That's the general idea. Why not? Do you turn into a pumpkin if you step foot off the enchanted grounds of dear old TPU?"

"Of course not. It's just that—I don't—I never—" She stopped and let out an exasperated breath. Try not to blither like an idiot, she told herself, and demanded out loud, "Is this a pickup?"

"Not so far, but only because I'm not being very successful at it," he admitted with disarming bluntness. "Would it help if I introduce myself? My name is Lee Michaels, and yours," he said, slipping a warm hand under her arm to pilot her toward the exit, "is Caitlin Stewart."

"How do you know that?" she asked, startled.

"I saw you standing next to the window and asked someone," he said simply. "You know, you're by far the prettiest woman in the room."

Caitlin was speechless. She considered herself moderately attractive. Her legs were long for her height and the parts of her face were assembled in a slightly irregular but arresting way, if one happened to like big hazel eyes and a tip-tilted nose. Her own preference would have been for shapelier curves and higher cheekbones, so she was stunned that this gorgeous man was as struck with her looks as she was with his.

Incorrigible honesty made her wonder if that was the only reason she was allowing him to tow her along. She was familiar with defense mechanisms and had had ample opportunity over the years to study her own. Perhaps her subconscious was trying to short-circuit the painful memories this party aroused by tempting her into unfamiliar conduct. Caitlin hadn't been coy when she said she didn't indulge in pickups. The stark fact was that since Jim's death she hadn't gone out with a man under any circumstances.

She caught her breath as they passed the coatrack. "Lee, look—"

"Is one of these yours?"

"The white sweater coat, but really I shouldn't just walk out. I haven't spoken to President Silverthorne yet and—"

"Don't let that bother you. I heard him say he was going to sneak out about fifteen minutes ago. So we won't be offending anybody." He draped the sweater around her neck.

"But, Lee—"

"Nope." Was the man never to let her finish a sentence? "You want to do a good deed, don't you? The least a nice girl like you could do is rescue a poor, misplaced person from all that genteel chitchat."

Caitlin looked up at him curiously. "You haven't told me what you were doing at a university function. Are you a new employee?" She knew she'd never seen him before.

"Not exactly," he answered vaguely. "I'm sort of assigned to TPU on a temporary basis."

That sounded safe, Caitlin thought with relief. No matter how compelling his gaze or how broad his shoulders, he couldn't do her self-possession much harm if he wasn't staying on campus long. After having grown up on the move as an Air Force brat, she valued the stability of Tall Pines. The university offered the kind of permanence an intelligent woman craved in an uncertain world.

"Anyway," he went on, ushering her out of the administration building, "I don't know Spokane very well. Where's a nice place to have a quiet drink?"

She stopped so suddenly at the top of the steps that they collided. Lee shot out an arm made of iron to sweep her back from the precipitous drop.

"Oh!" Heart clammering, she instinctively clutched him above the elbows. Sheer surprise kept her there. She knew almost to the day how long it was since she'd been in a man's arms. Was this what she'd been missing?

His male smell—after-shave and sun-dried cotton, underlaid by the deeply exciting musky scent of his skin—filled her head and set it swimming. If he'd moved his arms, she would have fallen straight down the granite steps to the brickwork below.

Lee was astounded. It couldn't be this easy.

From the first moment he'd seen her, taking tiny, suspicious sips of that poisonous mixture of formaldehyde and caramel coloring that TPU's purchasing department called wine, she'd intrigued him. There was something valiant and a little forlorn in the way she stood all alone. No woman with Titian hair and a kissable mouth and eyes of such a soft hazel they were gold should have been isolated at a party; either there was something severely wrong with the men at TPU or her air of being self-contained fooled them into believing only ice lay beneath it. Somehow, Lee was sure the fire that glowed in all that red hair had an echo in her nature.

She was completely unlike the female barracudas who'd taught him to be a realist about his looks.

Lee had enjoyed considerable, if brief, success in a career that drew aggressive women like flies, and even after an injury had forced him into another line of work, they had still swarmed.

Nothing about Caitlin was predatory. She was small and pert and ever so slightly wary. He liked that. And although an instinct honed by years of pursuit told him she was susceptible to the genetic coincidence that had produced his good looks, she wasn't obvious about it.

Until now. She was aware of him as she stood in the circle of his arms. He had too much experience to mistake her response. Her slight, light-boned body felt soft and somehow plush. He didn't want to let her go.

Who could have predicted he'd have cause to be grateful for the damned overhandsomeness that had dogged his image of himself ever since he could remember?

But it was too soon, too quick. His plans included meeting Caitlin Stewart, and if necessary cultivating her, but he hadn't counted on this instant liking, the reaction of his flesh to her touch. She made him feel like . . . Lord, what? A teenager. The kind of churning going on in his gut was certainly something he'd imagined left behind in adolescence.

Qualms assailed him. What was she going to say when she found out his reason for coming to Tall Pines? He had the uneasy feeling that sex would be a complicating, not a smoothing, factor in working with Coach Stewart's widow.

Proceed with caution, he thought.

Lee pulled her away from the edge and carefully released her. "My God, woman, we could have been nothing but a smear on the quad. Are you all right?"

Caitlin assured him breathlessly that she was fine, when another voice spoke over her shoulder.

"Well, Mrs. Stewart, Mr. Michaels, good afternoon."

President Silverthorne smiled at them benevolently, his gaze from behind thick trifocals shrewd.

Lee smiled easily. "Hello again, sir. Great weather. I haven't seen such glorious fall colors since I moved to San Francisco."

Silverthorne brightened. "Yes indeed, we're very proud of the variety of maples to be seen around campus. They're older trees, you know, many more than seventy years old, and require a good deal of expense for maintenance, but are well worth the effort. Alumni are always nostalgic about them. And that—" unexpectedly he laughed "—is good for donations. Now San Francisco is pleasant in its way, but not, *not* Spokane, Washington."

"That's very true," Lee murmured, making Caitlin inspect him narrowly. Spokane was a typical American small city, full of fast food and friendly people. Sprawling across a saucer-shaped valley between the Columbia Plateau and the Bitterroot Range, it notably lacked the glitter of San Francisco.

But if Lee was poking fun, it was of a very gentle variety. Caitlin owed a lot to Silverthorne, who'd rallied the resources of the university around Coach Stewart's family after his fatal heart attack. But even apart from the debt of gratitude she felt she owed him, Caitlin was fond of her employer, and she warmed to Lee.

Those blue eyes were certainly expressive. . . .

The great man then bade them goodbye, and she collected herself to answer in kind.

"Now," said Lee, "where do you want to go?"

"Lee, I have to go back inside. I've been trying to tell you, I came with somebody." Caitlin felt distinctly guilty because, for a few minutes, she'd forgotten completely. "I can't just leave without a word."

Lee's face remained perfectly composed and pleasant, but Caitlin found she couldn't look at it.

"I see. We'd better get you inside, then. Someone serious?"

He held the door for her again with an old-fashioned courtesy she liked very much.

"Serious?" she asked, mystified. "Oh—oh, no! Auretta works in acquisitions at the library. In fact, she sort of bullied me into coming to this reception. Under the circumstances it didn't appeal to me much. Football isn't exactly my life anymore, and frankly I can hardly even bear to think about it since all the corruption in the team has come to light. Thank God it all happened after Jim . . . was gone. If overwork hadn't killed him, the scandal would have. He loved the team." She added in explanation, "My husband, I mean. He used to coach football here."

The hallway to the reception room was long and empty, and as they walked along it, their steps mingled and echoed in a kind of tap dance. Caitlin's heart seemed to pick up the syncopation, making it difficult to breathe.

Lee looked straight ahead. "And just how do you perceive the problem the team's been having?"

"Well . . ." She hesitated. "You know about all the violations?" How could he help it? They'd been on sports pages all over the country.

"The bare bones, at least."

Caitlin could hear distaste sharpen her normally cheerful voice. "Alumni boosters paying students not to work, providing expensive gifts and vacations—hiring cheerleaders, for heaven's sake, to go out with potential recruits! If you want to put it nicely, there's been a tremendous amount of subsidizing going on. It's not easy to attract first-rate players out to the boonies when there are bigger-name schools in our conference promising more glory and better scholarships, but there must be ways short of bribery. Jim certainly never approved of anything like it."

"You think the current coach knew and didn't act until the mess went public?"

Caitlin shrugged. "I haven't the faintest idea. The rumor is that a fan broke the story. If the coach knew and didn't do anything, well, that makes him guilty, too, doesn't it?"

"A sin of omission, in other words."

"If you like."

They reached the threshold of the reception room and Caitlin craned her neck for a glimpse of her friend. "Auretta's kind of hard to miss. She's wearing a purple and orange handwoven shawl."

When they found Auretta, Caitlin planned to ease away from Mr. Lee Michaels and lose him in the crowd still gathered around the bar. He was dangerously attractive for a widow who had no intention of succumbing to his impulses. Or her own, for that matter. The sexual shock she'd received when she touched him still jangled along her nerves.

From his greater height, Lee said, "I see something that might fit your description. Good Lord, yes, you weren't kidding, were you? It really is purple and orange."

As a bulky figure not quite overwhelmed by fuzzy yards of alternating color clashed toward them, Caitlin murmured, "They are the school colors, you know. Auretta's, uh, patriotic."

Lee's face was alight with laughter as Auretta pushed her way up to them, so perhaps it wasn't surprising that she looked awestruck. Caitlin felt amused sympathy as she made the introductions. If Auretta's expression was any guide, her own reaction to Lee was not abnormal. He was a dazzling man.

Auretta was burbling away, but that wasn't unusual, either. Auretta always burbled.

"And I was so pleased when they announced that *you're* going to investigate our troubles. It wasn't so long ago that you had your wonderful season with the Bay City Barbarians, before that horrible accident. How is your knee, by the way? Really, it seems so providential that someone who actually understands the game will be handling this terrible mess, and, well, I'm just so pleased!"

Auretta and Lee took a breath at the same time. Lee spoke a microsecond before Auretta could inhale enough oxygen to fuel another statement.

"Thank you. I'm pleased myself. The conference considers this an important investigation."

Auretta nodded enthusiastically. "The powers that be could not have made a better choice. And it's so terrific to see you and Caitlin getting along just as if—as if—" She faltered to a stop. "Caitlin, honey, why are your eyes popping out?"

Caitlin had to clear her throat before any sound came out. "Lee," she said ominously.

She prided herself on maintaining a pretty even keel these days. The hasty temper that went with her red hair was something she'd never liked in herself. So conscious was she of its warning signs that in the years since she'd reached adulthood it rarely surfaced. Now she heard a certain note in her voice, felt the scald of a flush and a tightening along her jaw. She braced herself to ignore the symptoms. A professional academic librarian didn't make scenes in public—especially not at faculty receptions where people she intended to work with for the duration of her career would overhear and memorize every juicy tidbit, continuing to chew it over up to and including her retirement dinner. A true professional, unflappable to the core, would assess the situation, compute her options and do what any

woman with a healthy instinct for survival would do—
get as far away from Lee Michaels as quickly and as
permanently as possible.

A football conference investigator? she fumed. The
investigator digging into the muck surrounding the
team that had once been Jim's? That cozy drink was
undoubtedly part of the investigation. She felt the flush
rise in her cheeks again.

"Ah, yes," Lee said. "Look, Miss—okay, Auretta—I
was just trying to pry Caitlin out of here for a little private talk. Do you need a ride? Is there someplace we
could drop you off?" he added, making his meaning
clear.

Caitlin shot a look of pure entreaty at Auretta, which
her friend basely ignored.

"Now, isn't that a coincidence? I ran into a dear old
soul, sixty if he's a day, but then so am I, from the
physics department, and he asked me to check over
some equations with him. But I had to turn him down
because I came to this shindig with Caitlin here, and if
you think a man likes being left in the lurch at a party,
you should see what happens when a female deserts the
girl she came with—"

"Yes," said Caitlin inaudibly.

"So this works out perfectly for me, and I can tell it
does for you, too, what did you say, dear?"

Caitlin found it impossible to say anything, but
waved a wan hand as Auretta disappeared into the
crowd.

Lee grinned. "Let's get out of here before we're corralled again."

Caitlin maintained a stony silence until she was
seated beside Lee in the yielding leather of a custom-

made bucket seat. She'd never even heard of the make of his car, but it was long, low to the ground and decidedly exotic in comparison to the sensible compacts that filled the rest of the faculty parking lot. The sustained whoosh with which it backed up and then hummed out of the lot told her that Lee's car, like Lee, had more than just good looks. The machine was alive with power.

"Nice little car," she said.

He slid her a sideways glance. "It runs."

"I drive a '54 Mercedes."

"Nice little car," he repeated gravely.

Caitlin burst out, "I really don't want to have a drink with you."

His knuckles whitened as his hands clenched the wheel. "That's admirably direct. Are you always that to the point?"

His voice was even, but Caitlin felt a pang of remorse. After all, she'd gotten into the man's car without any sign of unwillingness. He had every right to expect minimal courtesy, or at least for her to refrain from downright insult.

"It's not you particularly," she said, not very coherently. "That is, it's not that I don't like you, because under different circumstances I would." And that was true, she thought with a sense of panic. She'd never felt such an instantaneous attraction to any man before, not even Jim. Deliberately she concentrated on Jim. "But frankly, I'm not interested in seeing anyone right now. I only recently lost my husband."

Lee's baritone developed an edge. "Recently? You are the widow of Jim Stewart, the football coach, aren't you? Seems to me he died about three years ago."

She gasped. When she could swallow the fury clogging her throat, she asked, "Is brutal honesty your specialty, Mr. Michaels?"

"It was my impression that it's usually yours, Mrs. Stewart." His stiff shoulders, only inches from her own, relaxed by what looked like an effort of will. "Maybe we should start all over again. How do you do? I'm Lee. I'd very much like to take you out and engage in a little civilized conversation over drinks. Who knows, we could even go all the way on our first date and share a hamburger or something."

"Lee—"

"You're supposed to say, 'I'm Caitlin.' Or do you have a nickname you prefer?"

"Not really. Caitlin is fine, except you don't need me to tell you my name. You already know it. You knew it when you picked me out of the crowd at the reception, and the reason you did it isn't because you thought I was—pretty—" her voice mocked him, and herself for believing him "—but because I used to be married to Jim Stewart. You think you can use me to find out things about the team."

The car was purring over brick streets dimmed to twilight by rows of fine old trees boasting patches of autumn foliage. Now and then a single bright leaf, flickering like a candle flame in the semidarkness, would drift across the windshield.

"That's not true," he said quietly. "Or rather, it's a distortion of the truth. Yes, I did know who you were, not just your name, and yes, I do mean to talk with you about the little problem TPU's been having with its recruiting policies. But no, I don't ordinarily pick up or hit on or whatever unpleasant phrase you care to choose, with witnesses in an investigation. For one thing, the witnesses I generally get stuck with are burly guys with beer bellies. For another, I don't care to spend my salary softening up informants."

"You mean they actually talk to you of their own free will?" she asked tightly.

"Frequently. Of course, I occasionally get someone else to apply a little handy coercion."

"Thumbscrews? The rack?"

"The iron maiden," he muttered, his narrowed eyes glinting blue at her. "Nothing so hackneyed, I imagine. I don't know for sure, but Silverthorne impresses me as the kind of president who can get his subordinates to do what he wants without having to turn to the messier medieval methods of intimidation."

"That's what you think. There's no place on earth as medieval as a college campus. Let me get this straight. President Silverthorne—"

"He said you'd be more than happy to cooperate with the conference investigation. He seemed to think you'd be pounding down my door, lobbying to make sure Coach Stewart's name stays clean."

Lee risked another glance at her. With the vivacity drained from her pointed face and the small, shapely mouth pressed in an unforgiving line, she actually looked feral. Whatever he'd aroused here, it wasn't what he'd been hoping for. The softness and pliancy were gone as if he'd only dreamed them.

The little mouth bit the words off one by one. "My husband doesn't require defending, Mr. Michaels, because he never in his life committed an improper act."

"Be realistic, Caitlin. Nobody's perfect. We all have a few human imperfections. Thank God. Listen, I'd really like to go out with a pretty woman and unwind a bit. I drove up from San Francisco overnight and spent most of the day in meetings. Dinner, a glass of wine—real wine—we could talk. Not about the past or the future, just about *this*." He reached over and put one tanned hand over hers. The current that ran between them was as tangible as an electric shock.

She snatched her hand away as if she'd been burned. "I already told you, I don't date."

"Caitlin, you can't tell me you don't feel something when we touch."

Lee eased the car to the curb and brought it to a halt without switching off the ignition. Earnestly he said, "Believe it or not, I don't normally force myself on unwilling women. But every instinct I've got is crying out that you're as attracted to me as I am to you. I don't usually go this fast, but I'm afraid if I let you go now you'll decide I'm some kind of monster with an ego problem. Assuming you haven't come to that conclusion already."

"I don't think you're a monster," said Caitlin. She was nursing her hand against her ribs.

"I could understand if you were anti-man—"

"For pity's sake!" she snapped. "It's not a question of being anti-man. I'm simply anti-football."

That was close enough to the truth, she assured herself. She wasn't anti-man. She was anti-hurt.

"That's a rather sweeping statement. Football aside—"

Caitlin ground her teeth. "We can't put it aside. It's a stupid, destructive, meaningless game. You're here because of football. It's your job. Auretta said you used to be a player. . . ."

There was real amusement in his grin. "Never heard of me, have you?"

"Well, I'm sorry—"

"Don't be. It's actually rather refreshing. I'm not such a jerk that I expect everybody in the world to remember I quarterbacked one season of pro ball. It's just a piece of sports trivia."

"You were injured?" she asked in a suddenly small voice.

"My knee was cracked up in the last game of the season." He saw her looking back and forth from one of his pant legs to the other and said gently, "It's not that big a deal. I can walk. I don't even limp anymore. Swimming helps quite a bit. I put in an hour at the pool every night when I can."

"It—it must have been a horrible jolt, losing your position on a pro team."

"Just the way the world works, honey." His shrug was philosophical. "The only thing I wonder at is that your pal Auretta didn't din my record into your ears." He added temperately, "She seems to like to talk."

"She may have tried to. I don't listen when people talk football. I sound hopelessly prejudiced, don't I? It's just that—" She felt a need to justify herself to this man. "It's just that Jim literally worked himself to death and for what? An essentially dumb game. Who cares whether the ball goes between the goalposts? It's just a ball. The stupid thing isn't even round. The whole game is an excuse for a lot of grown men who ought to know better to knock one another down. I can't—now I've insulted you again, haven't I?"

"Let's just say you have a unique talent for mashing a guy's ego down to size."

"Your ego, Lee? How about my feelings? You just happen not to mention you're a snoop for the football conference while you coincidentally ask me out for a friendly drink. For some strange reason I can't even understand, I'm here in this car with you—"

"Can't you?"

Lee's softly voiced question brought her rush of words to a stop. He leaned over and, very lightly, put his hand against her cheek. Using every ounce of her willpower, Caitlin stayed still under the contact, only swallowing convulsively to show how it affected her. Gently, as if to take the sting out of the remark, he said, "President Silverthorne told me you'd be one of the brightest people I'd meet at TPU. But a lot of things don't seem to be registering with you today."

Holding her breath for a moment and then letting it out in a long, cleansing exhalation sometimes worked to help Caitlin control her temper. Not this time.

Three years might be long by some measures, but when she thought back on them they were a blur of graduate school, learning a new job, holding down the fort at home.... Now, at last, just when she had achieved a sense of peace, of balance in her roles at the library and at home, this complete stranger blasted all her hard-earned serenity with a touch of his hand. She didn't want his understanding, or the sexual tingle that whispered of the excitement of risk to the blood rushing along her veins. Risk-taking was fine for people who didn't have to stick around and pick up the pieces of shattered dreams. Not for her. Loyalty might be shrugged off as inconvenient to a young widow meeting an attractive man. Not by her.

The anger helped. It brought her chin up proudly as she said, "If you take the next turn, we'll go right by my house. Then you can let me out and you won't have to put up with my unintelligent company anymore."

"Caitlin, please—"

"And I won't have to put up with yours."

Lee wrenched the wheel but the car was so well made it only rocked lightly on its springs as it rounded the corner.

"If that's what you want," he said.

"Definitely."

"Then it's my pleasure." Rubber burned as he braked savagely. "Goodbye, Mrs. Stewart."

2

CAITLIN SLAMMED the door of her house and then
screamed under her breath for good measure. She
couldn't remember having been so mad since—since—
she couldn't remember *ever* having been so mad. Of all
the arrogant, deceitful, know-it-all males on the face
of the earth, Lee Michaels was the A-number-one ab-
solute worst.

Ego problem! The only problem with his ego was
that it was big enough to swallow all of eastern Washington, plus the Cascades, plus . . .

Caitlin stomped into the kitchen. Maybe she'd find
something to break in there. Instead she found her
stepson, Toby, elbows sprawled across the table, hands
clutching an impossibly thick sandwich.

"What's that?" Caitlin demanded. "It looks terrible.
Sit up straight, you look like a big gorilla."

"Ung," said Toby. He chewed vigorously and swallowed. "Hi, Ma. What's up? You've got sparks flying
from your hair."

For an instant, Caitlin teetered on the brink of a really
satisfying temper tantrum. Then her good humor as-
serted itself, and she burst into laughter. "No, do I? I felt
like it, for a minute."

"Party get too bad? It sounded like a bummer."
Awkwardly, he added, "I know people are starting to
say that Dad—"

The strain in his newly deepened voice tore at her heart. Briefly she considered finding the idiots who'd said such a thing to Jim's son and rending them limb from limb. Instead, she interrupted with ruthless cheerfulness. "What is in that repulsive sandwich? You'll never eat your dinner."

"Liverwurst mostly." Toby seemed happy to abandon a taboo subject. "Can't stay for dinner, anyway. I'm going to Brenda's."

Caitlin knew all about Brenda. Toby had talked about her, to the exclusion of almost any other topic except forms of transportation—cars, dirt bikes, eighteen-speed bicycles—since the beginning of his senior year of high school. The two of them were entering the freshman class at TPU in a couple of days. Caitlin suspected that Brenda, an undoubted brain, had turned down a number of flattering scholarship offers from other schools to remain close to Toby.

"I don't suppose I can borrow the car tonight?" he asked, interrupting her thoughts and giving her a winning smile.

She smiled back. "Under no circumstances. The car will be yours when you graduate from college. Not a minute sooner."

He sighed. "That's what I thought." Crumbling the crust of his sandwich, he asked, "Ma, what would you do if—if it turns out that—if Dad..." He ran out of words.

Protective affection flooded her. "Toby, we both know what kind of man your dad was. Nothing anybody says can change the truth."

"The truth. Yeah."

The look on his face was still too thoughtful, but he planted a kiss somewhere near her left ear and shot out the door. She heard him singing tunelessly as he rattled his bike out of the garage and sped away. Toby was saving to restore an old junk heap that lacked, among other things, a working transmission.

The mail was stacked on the counter. It included a note from personnel. Since Mrs. Stewart had failed to respond to previous notifications that her accrued vacation time exceeded the maximum permitted, the director would regretfully be obliged to disallow the excess days unless Mrs. Stewart took a vacation immediately.

Immediately was underlined in red.

One of these days, Caitlin thought, she'd have to get out to the cabin and close it up for the winter, but she'd hardly require vacation time to do it. She crumpled the notice.

"Use it or lose it," she said aloud. "Big deal."

Slowly she pulled a mug from the cupboard and made tea. She sat down to enjoy the fragrance and take an occasional sip, her thoughts revolving unhappily around Lee Michaels.

The anger she tried to summon had dwindled to embarrassment. Why had she let him affect her so?

Three years of evading the wolves on the faculty ought to have left her in better practice. Of course, Lee was an entirely different caliber of wolf. There were an awful lot of Ph.D.s infesting the campus who suffered from the erroneous impression that a degree magically endowed them with sex appeal. She had to admit that Lee, whatever his educational background, wasn't suffering from any misapprehensions in that regard. He really did have sex appeal.

Well, she might not be able to avoid him completely—Tall Pines wasn't a big campus—but the next time her path crossed his, she'd be cool, polite and distant. Very distant, she decided, remembering the strength in his arms, the way he smelled, how he breathed. Her hands actually trembled as they closed around the mug. If her traitorous body was going to go so—so liquid every time Lee Michaels touched her, she'd just have to make sure he never got near enough to complete contact. All her sweet, womanly feelings were buried in the grave with Jim, and she wasn't going to risk exhuming them.

Jim had had laughing blue eyes, too.

A year of chaste not-quite-dates had led up to their wedding soon after her graduation. Plans for a honeymoon were postponed and postponed again as the demands of his position as head coach disrupted all her hopes for a normal married life. For months Jim had practically lived at the university.

Drunk with love for the very first time, Caitlin had accepted as patiently as she could, that her adored husband was not much more than a nearly invisible presence slipping late at night into bed to engage in bouts of lovemaking as if, she had thought at the time with wry amusement, what happened between them was another athletic event on his busy schedule. It left her satisfied in body but increasingly frustrated in mind. She wanted a companion, not just a midnight lover.

Only until the end of the season, Jim had promised. They'd have a chance to do things together at the end of the season.

His season ended in October with a massive heart attack. Caitlin was left, still in love, with the feeling her marriage had only been half-consummated, and with a fifteen-year-old stepson she barely knew.

Caitlin started. For an instant she imagined she could hear a younger Toby, still a soprano, shrieking for her out of one of his devastating nightmares.

The sound was repeated.

"Oh, Lord," Caitlin said. "Flame, where are you?"

Hard nails scrabbled close by.

"There goes the varnish." Muttering to herself, Caitlin went to the back door. Before she could open it more than two inches, a sinuous shape slunk through the crevice and wrapped itself around her ankles.

Caitlin scooped up the velvety, pillowy weight. Flame butted her narrow Siamese head against Caitlin's cheek. Her slow, rhythmic purr sounded like the steady beat of an engine in Caitlin's ear.

Who needed a man—any man, she thought—when she could have a cat instead?

"And where have you been, huh?" Caitlin asked, nuzzling the aristocratic pink nose with her own. "Out making yourself obnoxious to the neighborhood, I bet. Did you catch anything disgusting? Are you hungry?"

Flame slid from her hands to investigate her Wedgwood bowl, which still contained some dry food from breakfast. While she crunched enthusiastically, Caitlin refilled a matching bowl with fresh water.

The porcelain was a present from Toby.

Caitlin wondered what other boy would have spent his own money, saved from a so-so allowance and the slim profit he made cutting lawns all summer, on such an imaginative gift. Maybe one existed somewhere, but Toby was hers. Her responsibility for a little while yet.

He'd said, "Ma, it's crazy for me to move to a dorm when I can live at home. Tall Pines is giving me free tuition because of Dad, so we can save a bundle. I'd rather live at home, honest!"

So, here we are, she thought, swirling the tea in her mug, still bound together by Jim. And by Tall Pines.

The tea was cold. Caitlin rinsed the cup and wandered into the living room with Flame in her arms. A portrait of Jim, smiling steadily into the camera, was surrounded by other family pictures on one wall.

"Oh, Jim," she whispered, "why couldn't I make you love me enough to stay home and put your feet up once in a while? Why did you push yourself and push yourself until—"

She broke off. The words formed in her mind anyway—*until your heart burst*.

With a sigh, she shook off the old, guilt-tinged memories and deposited Flame on the couch. What was the matter with her today? She didn't usually drift aimlessly from room to room, talking to pictures on the walls, dwelling on long-past events she knew perfectly well ought to be forgotten.

The answer that occurred to her—that it wasn't every day she met a man with Technicolor good looks and a zippy sports car, who made her feel emotions she didn't want to feel, refused to feel—Caitlin dismissed at once. After all, she'd never been overly impressed with glamorous externals. No one would have described

Jim's blunt-featured sandiness, which Toby had inherited, as handsome, and she'd loved him dearly.

Maybe it wasn't Lee's dark-hawk splendor that attracted her, she decided reluctantly. More likely, and more dangerous, were the laughter and sympathy that lurked behind the brilliance of his eyes. As if he might understand the bone-chilling loneliness of an unshared bed and the failure of love to drive away death. Caitlin's relationship to Toby was carefully mother to son, despite, or because of, the slim difference in their ages. Much as she loved him, there were topics she simply couldn't discuss with him.

Like the aches of the flesh and the soul.

One thing she could never bring up with him was this disconcerting rapport with a total stranger. A stranger who was investigating Toby's father for bribery and corruption. A stranger whose first and second careers were *football*.

It might not be reasonable—it might not even be very bright, as Lee had told her ever so gently that afternoon—but Caitlin didn't care. She was never, never again going to get involved with a man whose life revolved around football.

With a tired groan, she realized her reverie had come full circle. She was still thinking about Lee Michaels.

Outside the fall day was deepening into night. Through the window, sunset backlit a lacy network of twigs and leaves where trees raised buoyant limbs to the sky.

Caitlin loved this room. Windows facing south and west let in light all day, while the tall coved ceiling kept the temperature pleasantly cool during the hot, dry summers. A large fireplace with an unobtrusive insert provided cheer during cold months. Caitlin decided it was time to order a cord of wood. Without Flame generating heat in her arms, it was definitely chilly.

She watched the afterglow of day dim and vanish. Even after the shadowy trees blended into the night, she stood drained of thought, suspended between the darkness of the empty room and the blackness outside.

The afternoon had been full of too many emotions. Right now she didn't want to feel anything. A shoe scuffled on the cement walk that led to the house, sounded on the steps to the front porch. Caitlin vaguely hoped that whoever it was would just go away.

The doorbell chimed. Normally it had a mellow sound, but now it struck her as shrill, jarring her out of whatever spell was making her part of the night. With a sudden shiver that brought all her senses awake, Caitlin went to answer it.

"Hi." The deep monosyllable came out of the darkness. Lee. "You forgot this in my car."

It was a moment before Caitlin's finger found the switch that controlled the porch light. The yellow bulb high in its carriage lamp revealed a purse dangling ridiculously from Lee's large male hand.

"Oh," she said blankly. "Stupid of me. I didn't notice it was gone."

Lee looked past her into the hall. "Nice place."

"Thank you."

The silence stretched out one minute, then two. Lee, damn him, wore a bland look that promised infinite patience.

Reluctantly Caitlin said, "Come on in."

When he followed her into the living room, she resented the way his presence filled the space.

"Tea?" she offered tersely, hoping he'd turn it down.

Instead, he settled himself on the sofa, legs extended to their considerable length and crossed at the ankles, like a man who intended to stay a while. "Sounds great," he answered, his gaze resting on her battery of photographs.

For some reason she didn't try to fathom, Caitlin chose the good china for her unwanted guest. She took a good long time to steep the tea and arrange a tray with milk, lemon and sugar. When she returned, Lee stood to take the cup and saucer, indicating the picture of Jim.

"That's a great shot. It gives you a real feeling for what he must have been like."

The candid photograph caught Jim at practice, big and bluff and fully alive.

"Thanks. I took it the year before we got married. The school paper even used it for a feature story they ran on him."

"You were, what, twenty-three or so?"

She lifted her eyes quickly to his face, but his attention was fixed on the portrait.

"Twenty-two. And if you're thinking that Jim was older than I was," she flared, "it just didn't matter. We didn't know about his heart condition." Bringing her voice back under control, she added lightly, "After the funeral, I asked for the negative, and some earnest future archivist dug it out of the files for me. It enlarged really well, don't you think?"

"I like this one, too. Is that Jim's son with you?" Lee asked, moving on.

"Mmm-hmm. His high school graduation last June."

"What is he, nineteen?"

Caitlin shook her head. "Eighteen."

"A well-grown specimen," Lee said mildly.

"Well, I know there isn't much difference between Toby's age and mine," Caitlin admitted. "But after Jim's heart attack, it *felt* like more, somehow. Toby was pretty young for fifteen. He'd lost his mother in a car accident when he was ten. And the gap between fifteen and twenty-three is bigger than the one between eighteen and twenty-six. He's wonderful about letting me be his mom, though. Neither of us has anybody else, so we've just kept on being a family."

"No life of your own?" he asked.

Caitlin deliberately misunderstood. "I have a very nice life. President Silverthorne has been a godsend—he made sure TPU financed my master's degree and gave me a job in the library. Toby pays no tuition. If I want to go out, there's always a concert or play or lecture."

"Sounds exhilarating."

She bristled at his flat tone. "Lee, even if you don't like the amenities of academic life, lots of people do."

He shrugged. "I don't mind having my cultural horizons expanded once in a while. It's just that there are other things in life, too."

"Lee, I—"

He said steadily, "I could have returned your purse at work on Monday, but this gave me a chance to see you and apologize. Caitlin? I don't know everything that's going on with you, that's obvious. But if I came on too strong this afternoon—"

"Lee, it's all right, really. You don't need to apologize. There's nothing to be sorry for. There's just—nothing. Okay?"

His body was braced. Now his chin jerked back the tiniest bit, as if absorbing a blow.

"Yes, I see. Well, thanks for making it clear. I guess I've outstayed my welcome."

Caitlin trailed him to the door. It was kinder to end his interest in her now, she told herself, assuming real interest was what he felt, and only natural to feel awful about it. She did feel awful about it.

The screen creaked as Lee opened it, and something small at floor level flowed out toward freedom. Flame gave a chirrup of surprise at encountering feet and backed a few inches to cock her head up and survey the giant on her doorstep.

"What's this?" asked Lee in a more normal tone. "I've never seen a cat with this coloring before. What a beauty!"

Caitlin said, "She's a colorpoint shorthair, a mix of red tabby with Siamese. They're pretty rare. We were able to afford her because she's not show quality."

"She's not? Who would care? A white-and-orange Siamese!"

She laughed. "Well, it's never bothered us. But apparently it's a terrible flaw for her to have yellow eyes instead of blue." She couldn't help a quick glance at the only pair of blue eyes in the vicinity. "She'd never win any ribbons in competition with other red-points. Somewhere I came across another name for the variety—Flame Concha. It's kind of pretentious, but that's what we ended up calling her, anyway."

Lee put out his hand for Flame to sniff before he laid it across her back in a single gentle caress. He straightened and looked down at Caitlin. This warm, human girl was a far cry from the furious, infuriating woman who'd jumped out of his car this afternoon. The misery she'd tried so hard to hide as they stood in front of Jim Stewart's portrait still lingered in lines she was too young to have bracketing her mouth. He felt an irresistible impulse to erase them.

"I don't know. The name seems perfect to me. Copper hair, big golden eyes—they deserve a poetic description, don't you think?"

Caitlin smothered a gasp. "We were talking about the *cat*."

"So we were," he agreed gravely.

The pause that followed was filled with a million whispered voices Caitlin couldn't quite overhear. A slow drumroll started in her temples. Lee smiled meaninglessly and took a step backward. Caitlin watched him begin to walk away.

He turned on his heel, strode up the steps and pulled her into his arms.

"You know, cat eyes," he said, "I've always thought of myself as a pretty nice guy. But I guess not nice enough. I'll give you fair warning, though. If you don't want to be kissed, you'd better say something... right... now."

Caitlin's vocal chords were paralyzed. She wanted to say...what did she want to say? *No* shouldn't be too hard. It was a short, easy word. Somehow she couldn't force it past the contrary resolve, which seemed to be gripping her throat, to sigh *yes*.

She stood absolutely still, her gaze on a level with Lee's collarbone. He'd abandoned the jacket and tie he'd worn to the reception and thrown a rough-napped sweater over his open-necked shirt. Pushing out above the V she could see a small forest of short hair curling black against his skin.

Lee's first kiss fell on her temple, lightly drawing the pain away. As his lips moved over her forehead, a weight seemed to press down on her eyelids. With eyes closed, she could feel each touch tingle against her waiting nerve ends. This was torture, exquisite and timeless. Her lips opened in a silent cry. Finally, he lowered his mouth to hers.

She was aware of nothing but the kiss until his tongue flicked out to capture hers. A moan escaped her. Desire kindled in places anesthetized far too long.

Lee hadn't intended more than a quick and, he hoped, mutually satisfactory kiss. He was afraid Caitlin wasn't ready for anything else. She was too unsure of him, maybe of herself, for bolder love play.

But when her lips softened and parted under his, it seemed natural, inevitable, for his tongue to seek the moist heat of hers. And the tiny moan pleasure wrung from her throat undid him.

His hands had been sliding gently from her elbows to her shoulders. Now one reached behind to give comforting support to muscles that were suddenly soft as butter, while the other drifted inside the muffling folds of her suit jacket. His fingertips, light and assured, traced the contours of her waist, and to Caitlin it felt as if the material of her blouse wasn't even there. And his mouth—she'd never really thought of mouths as organs of pleasure before—his mouth singed a trail of fire to the unguarded skin at the base of her throat.

He lifted his head. "I can't figure out if you're a witch sent to bedevil me, or a witch's familiar," he said hoarsely, but with a hint of laughter. "Hellcat. Don't you think we'd better stop this or go inside to discuss it further? My own vote's for inside. What will your neighbors say?"

Reality crashed in on Caitlin with the stinging force of a bucketful of cold water. The neighbors could say whatever they wanted; she didn't care. But what if Toby were to come home suddenly? He'd idolized his father. And here was his father's wife, not with just any man, but with the football conference investigator who'd had the gall to question Jim's honesty only hours before.

She whispered, "No. Oh, no. I can't. I'm sorry, Lee."

The color in his lean cheeks darkened to a brown stain, and Caitlin braced herself for anger, but he said ruefully, "It's all right, honey. I shouldn't have moved in on you so fast. It was my fault."

"You don't understand—"

"I do. You need some time to decide if I'm an egomaniac or a sex maniac or just a maniac."

"*No.* Time won't help," she said desperately. How could she break through Lee's relentless reasonableness? "I just plain can't!"

Lee ran a palm over his jaw. "Can't? Caitlin, forgive me, but you've been giving a rather convincing impression of a woman who could and would. This is the second time today you've responded and then frozen up. Okay, you're free to give or withdraw your favors as you see fit. But for God's sake, you blow hot and cold like a—a faulty furnace. I'm a simple guy. I can't keep up." He touched her hair fleetingly, in a gesture of—reassurance? Appeal? "Even if it is too soon, we've got to talk."

Caitlin stared at the porch floor. "Please just leave me alone. Completely alone."

Lee said grimly, "All right, Garbo. I'm going. Call me when—if—you decide what you want."

His quick steps faded into the night. Caitlin eased the door shut and twisted the lock.

3

CAITLIN CRAWLED into bed early and supperless, counting the hours as sleep rolled further and further away. By midnight she was wide awake, mind in turmoil and body aching with longings aroused and unsatisfied. Damn Lee Michaels, anyway, she thought. No man had the right to be that sexy.

Finally, unable to bear the quiet room, she kicked off the covers, threw on her robe and padded downstairs.

There was some rum in the cabinet under the kitchen sink, which she used mainly to flavor chocolate balls at Christmas; she poured a dollop into a tumbler with orange juice and slumped with it in front of the television. Using the remote control impatiently, she clicked through the channels till she found an old movie.

Fred and Ginger twirled and preened, their love a dance that needed no rehearsal. Their effortless pairing flickered across the screen, shadowy and unreal. Usually she loved musicals, with their elegant stars and unabashedly romantic plots. Not tonight.

"So why am I watching?" Caitlin asked herself. The empty house didn't answer.

The drink revived her appetite, and she sliced some cheese to go with crackers. Fred and Ginger danced off into the credits.

One-thirty. Sleep seemed as far off as ever, so she made herself another drink, weaker this time. An endless stream of commercials followed the movie. A switch to one of the pay channels revealed a half-naked barbarian with improbably greaseless hair. Her repulsion at his grotesquely inflated musculature only reminded her of Lee's arm wrapped around her. Somehow she imagined his biceps hard with the slim muscles that came from real exertion, not steroids and exercise machines.

Caitlin said, "Oh, please," and shut off the set.

Toby wandered in. Hands in pockets, he rocked on his heels as he smiled guilelessly at her. "Hi, Ma. A little late for you to be up, isn't it?"

"Don't be impertinent. That's my line. Surely you haven't been at Brenda's all this time?"

"Oh, there was a party at somebody's house. It's still going on, but I came on home 'cause I knew you'd be worried."

"Very virtuous," Caitlin approved. "Have you been drinking? Or anything else?"

Toby grimaced. "Uh, well, yeah. Just two beers. *Light* beers, honest. And I didn't drive."

"I know you didn't. I have the car. Where's your bike?"

"At Brenda's. I can walk over and get it tomorrow. No problem. You going to be mad at me, Ma?"

"I can't work up the strength tonight. Try me in the morning."

"It is morning. Besides, what's that you've got? Kind of a funny color for orange juice, little stepmother."

Caitlin shook her head. "Got me. Sleeping potion. It hasn't worked, though. I'm going to take some acetaminophen and go to bed."

Toby said admiringly, "You said that very well. Ace-taminophen. Nobody would ever suspect you of being a solitary midnight drinker."

"That's why I said it."

"Me, too. Don't wake me up too early, okay? Maybe noon, or one. Or two. By the way, Ma, you don't have to worry about me being into anything illegal. You didn't raise me to be dumb."

"Oh, Toby, I love you so. Good night."

Caitlin did sleep, fitfully, and woke to the sound of Toby clattering around. Saturdays were casual at their house, since Caitlin saw little point in trying to impose mealtimes on a normal teenage male. Toby was on his own as long as the dishes made it into the sink and the lawn got cut or the sidewalk shoveled, depending on the season.

Sweeping back chintz curtains, Caitlin winced from the soft autumn sunlight. She felt hung over, more from the lack of rest than the moderate amount of alcohol she'd consumed.

A shower. A nice, scalding, soothing shower that went on and on until all the hot water was used up might restore her enthusiasm for living.

Leaving her floral-printed flannel nightgown in a heap on the linoleum, she stepped into the claw-footed tub and pulled the shower curtain completely around. The plumbing, including the shower-head itself and the pipe that served it, dated from two generations before. Caitlin didn't mind. Swathed in plastic, water rushing and stinging on her skin, she felt a kind of queenly isolation.

She loved this funny bathroom. She loved the whole house. Solid, old-fashioned, comfortable, safe. Steam filled her nostrils. On their marriage, Jim had encouraged her to repaint, repaper or recover every surface in her new home, and since she'd had little else to do, she'd made a thorough job of it. The result was a blend of soft country prints, misty with greens and blues, touched here and there with the palest of earth tones. Everywhere in the house she breathed peace.

The needles of water began to lose their white-hot edge. Caitlin sighed, shut off the faucets and reached for one of the huge, deep-piled bath sheets Jim had insisted upon. She rubbed her body with firm, downward strokes that brought the blood coursing through her fair skin.

Broiled and rubbed to a rosy glow, hair curling defiantly despite her halfhearted attempt to brush it smooth, Caitlin dragged on a pair of jeans and a particularly ratty sweatshirt that read, "Property of Tall Pines." Toby had disappeared by the time she made her way to the kitchen, so she contented herself with a solitary cup of coffee—decaf be damned, she thought—and then, screen door slamming behind her, went out to continue the cure with some fresh air.

It was a fine day, as crisp and colorful as the day before. Maples, ash and sumac enclosed a tunnel of older, well-tended homes. Just above eye level spread an endless patchwork of orange, red, brown and gold. Native pines thrust dark, acid-green fingers through the softer mass of deciduous trees. This unincorporated section of town clung to the freedom to burn fallen leaves, and richly scented smoke hung in the air.

Caitlin shrugged her shoulders into a bone-cracking stretch. Lee Michaels, she decided, for all his muscles

and his wooing blue eyes, was nothing but a temporary aberration in her settled, secure life.

Misery seeped away. Last night was banished, a
short-lived flutter of impulses that no longer had a focus, like the echo of pain in an amputated limb. Today
would be devoted to unruffled serenity, a little exercise
in the form of yard work, the resumption of the routine that never failed to soothe and reassure. Today and
tomorrow and the next day.

"The lady librarian is looking satisfied with herself," said her neighbor, Ed Mallory, who owned a big
department store downtown. He leaned on the handle
of his rake and grinned at her over the fence.

"Oh! Hi. I was just making my New Year's resolu-
tions early."

"Good for you! What have you resolved?"

"That would be telling," Caitlin heard herself say
coyly and groaned inwardly. Ed Mallory always had
this effect on her. Perhaps because she liked him so little, she found herself responding with the same arch-
ness he used. He was a hard-faced man, with an
unconvincing smile that revealed large teeth and fleshy
gums. His only passion, outside of inventory and the
minimum wage, was football.

During her marriage, he'd corralled her at every opportunity, trying for inside information, and she supposed he still did so out of habit. Since he was a good
friend to the university, donating conspicuously to
every fund drive, Caitlin tried to control her distaste.
At least none of the recent scandal had touched his
name. Although several of the alumni caught in the
scandal were cronies of his, Mallory hadn't been im-
plicated.

Edging closer, he said, "Glad I saw you, as a matter of fact. Wife's giving a little party tomorrow night, just drinks and dinner, thought you might be free?"

How many invitations from the Mallorys had she turned down in the past year? Caitlin asked herself. Two or three? Her relations with them might be tepid, but she preferred to stay on good terms with her neighbors. Besides she rather liked Ed's crushed-looking wife, who'd been unobtrusively kind during those first, worst, months of widowhood.

"How sweet of you to think of me," Caitlin said with as much warmth as she could muster. "Please tell Susanna I'd love to come. When should I be there?"

"Five, five-thirty. See you then!"

He trotted around the side of his house, holding the rake upright like a standard. The carpet of leaves over his lawn was undisturbed. How odd, Caitlin thought. It was almost as if the rake had been nothing but a prop, an excuse to run out and issue the impromptu invitation.

Perhaps someone had canceled at the last minute. Caitlin wondered about the look that had flashed across Ed's face as she accepted. Was it relief? It was hard to tell; his flattened features didn't record expressions very well.

Shrugging, Caitlin went to find her own lawn tools and tackle the leaves drifting across her property.

An hour later there was a satisfyingly large pile of dried vegetation sprawled over the bit of wasteland near the alley that she and Toby used for burning. Straightening to relieve the crick in her back, Caitlin pulled off her gardening gloves to hunt for blisters.

Happily none had formed, so she could survey her neat patch of yard with unalloyed pride.

The phone began to ring from inside the house. Dashing into the kitchen, Caitlin picked up the receiver and sang out, "Hello!"

"Hello to you, too! I can tell you're in a good mood!"

"Auretta. How are you?" Caitlin asked as she rummaged in the refrigerator. Her appetite was back, but Toby didn't seem to have left much for a late lunch.

"Not as well as you, I bet. Do you know, that old man from the physics department really did want me to check over his stupid equations? Not the math or whatever it is, but the article he's writing to go with it. Can you imagine? Did he get a piece of my mind!"

Caitlin couldn't help laughing. "Auretta, you shouldn't have. Did the poor man figure out it wasn't his brain you were interested in but his biomass?"

"Now, isn't that a genteel way of putting it? I haven't the foggiest idea. Well, professors! You just never know how bright they really are, do you?"

Caitlin thought of some of the instructors she dealt with at the library. "That's a fact. Listen, are you busy this afternoon? Want to go shopping or something and get some dinner? Somewhere far, far away from the science building?"

"That has real appeal, honey. Shall I pick you up or do you want to run by here?"

They settled on Caitlin's car, and soon the cream-colored Mercedes was threading its way through the harrowing system of one-way streets in downtown Spokane. New buildings jostled old in a pleasing miscellany. Many of the structures that predated skyscrapers had restored brick and ironwork facades.

Caitlin found a parking place near a converted warehouse that held a fashion boutique for small sizes.

"What are we looking for?" asked Auretta as they entered Debbie's Petite Boutique.

"A new slip. Remember that spaghetti sauce I spilled all over myself at the comptroller's retirement party? It went straight through. My best white slip now has a map of Great Britain down the front. Let's see. This is pretty, isn't it?"

"It's all right. Now *this*," said Auretta, brandishing a lace-adorned teddy, "is pretty!"

Caitlin abandoned a rack of functional undergarments to admire Auretta's choice. "You're right. But it's not terribly practical. You couldn't wear anything over that shade of aqua except that shade of aqua."

"Well, I saw something when we came into the shop—here! Try this! And this!"

Caitlin backed up, laughing, her arms jammed with clothes on hangers. "Wait a minute! I came in for a slip. This is not a major shopping expedition."

Auretta sighed. "You listen to me, Caitlin O'Malley Stewart. I'm telling you this for your own good. It's no use thinking you're going to keep the interest of a downright splendiferous creature like that Lee Michaels if you don't do something with yourself. Most of your clothes are positively orthopedic. I haven't seen you in one new thing since—well, for about three years now. Your wardrobe just shrieks maiden-lady librarian."

Caitlin said mildly, "I haven't been a maiden lady for some time now. I'm perfectly happy with the image I project. I am a librarian. I'm not a femme fatale."

"In that getup," said Auretta with devastating frankness, surveying Caitlin's simple beige skirt and sweater, "you're not femme at all. Tell me this. Were you planning to replace that dreary white blouse with the floppy bow? If memory serves, it got doused, too."

Caitlin felt absurdly guilty. "I didn't think I'd need to. I've got a blue turtleneck that goes with the same suit, so I was just going to wear—"

"That old thing! My grandma's corset cover's younger than that. We're going to find you some clothes designed in this quarter of the twentieth century. Debbie! Where is that woman?"

As Auretta plowed through the close-set racks, Caitlin tried to control a spurt of panic. She didn't want to be made over. Certainly not to impress a man she'd literally kissed goodbye less than twenty-four hours ago. But when Auretta returned, her plump hand steering the proprietor in Caitlin's direction, she felt her determination weakening. It had been a long time since she'd bothered with her appearance. She wasn't immune to the lure of new clothes. And the silhouette was different this year; she responded instinctively to the softer, tapering lines that would become her more than the austere linens and woolens she'd adopted as her work uniform.

With a sudden sense of adventure, Caitlin capitulated.

Auretta made the selections, strong colors and cuts so extreme that Caitlin protested once or twice, but in almost every case the older woman was proven right. The aquas, teals and russets she chose highlighted Caitlin's warm coloring, and Debbie assured her the unfamiliar shapes were the latest thing.

The only garment Caitlin wouldn't consider was a fluffy oversize dress that looked hideously impractical for work, or anything else Caitlin could think of. Auretta argued in vain.

"Well, you're right," she finally said with a sigh. "The look we want for you calls for something a lot more sexy."

Caitlin opened her hazel eyes indignantly, but before she could repudiate Auretta's choice of adjective, her friend raised her voice. "Debbie, I'm going to buy this for myself. You got it in a sixteen, honey?"

The long-suffering Debbie blanched. Today Auretta was packed into skintight pants with a short, furry jacket stolen from some unidentifiable but roly-poly animal. Her brassy hair was squashed under a bright orange cap. The thought of her stout, aggressive figure enlarged by the unstructured garment obviously appalled Debbie.

"I don't think so," she said in a dazed kind of way.

"You get one in, you let me know, hear?" Auretta winked at Caitlin, who was writing a check for an ungodly amount.

While they were struggling to the car with their burden of boxes and slippery plastic bags, Auretta asked cheerfully, "Getting late, isn't it? Too late to do anything about your hair today—"

"My *hair*?"

"I know the little squirt all the students go to—if they can afford him. Let's see if I can get him to take you tomorrow sometime."

"Auretta, tomorrow's Sunday! I've got to go to a neighbor's for dinner in the afternoon. Besides there's nothing wrong with my hair!"

Auretta gave her a long look, and Caitlin asked meekly, "Is there?"

"Let's just say it's not so much a matter of something wrong as nothing right. Do you have any change? Or— wait, I've got my dialing card." With a brisk competence that didn't surprise Caitlin, Auretta began dealing with the alarming complexities of a computerized pay phone.

She hung up and beamed. "He can't take you tomorrow, but they'll squeeze you in tonight, seein' as how you're an emergency case. We'll just have time for a nice supper. Where do you want to eat?"

"You mean I get to choose?"

"Now, Caitlin, don't get sarcastic. It's so unbecoming. Why don't we try that Cajun place where they give you a little Confederate flag in your drink?"

Caitlin nodded. "As long as it's not too terribly expensive. Do you know how much of my money we've spent already?"

"Oh, hon!" Auretta actually looked embarrassed. "I didn't even think. Are you broke?"

Laughing, Caitlin shook her head. "It's okay. What with my paycheck and the trust fund Jim set up for Toby and me, there's plenty if neither of us goes wild. At least not too often. I was just teasing."

"Humph. Just for that, you may buy the drinks. They charge the earth for those Confederate flags."

The food was spicy and good. Caitlin found herself giggling over Auretta's pungent remarks on her nonencounter with the physics professor. Once or twice the memory of her own far-different interlude with Lee Michaels—necking under the porch light like a pair of high school kids—sent an awakening vibration through parts of her anatomy she'd hoped had gone to sleep again. With an effort, she made herself concentrate on Auretta's entertaining monologue.

All too soon, it was time to drive to the hairdresser's.

"What's wrong with my hair?" Caitlin asked again. "Specify."

"You've worn it precisely the same way ever since I've known you. It droops. You hide behind it. It—"

"All right! I believe you. Gee."

Caitlin hesitated as Auretta swung the door of the hair salon outward and stood waiting in expressive silence. "You're not going to let them make me look like that, are you?" Caitlin pointed to the poster of a model who'd apparently had her hair styled by Dr. Seuss.

With a snort, Auretta propelled Caitlin into the stuffy, perfumed confines of the salon.

After a quick shampoo, Caitlin was told that Jacques wasn't quite ready, so Auretta, who'd followed her into the working area to cajole and supervise, suggested in swift succession a manicure, pedicure and facial.

"Absolutely not!" said Caitlin flatly. "I don't like goop on my nails. And the only time I ever used a face mask it left welts. My skin's too fair. So why don't you have the facial?" she asked craftily. "It'll relax you, open your pores. Pay you back for what you've been doing to me all afternoon."

She motioned to the skin care operator, who moved with alacrity to snare a customer. Auretta was pushed gently onto a chair that looked as if it belonged in a dental office and was hoisted aloft to have her complexion examined under a magnifying glass.

Auretta made a face at Caitlin. "You're not going to escape while I'm not looking, are you?"

"Don't be too sure," said Caitlin. She added to the cosmetician, "Give her the works."

Jacques appeared then and herded Caitlin toward the rear of the shop. He certainly wasn't French. In fact, his accent, with its pinched consonants and squared-off vowels, sounded as if it had been acquired somewhere near Baltimore. But he spoke with a great many Gallic flourishes and a distinct twinkle in his eye.

"Lovely, lovely!" he crooned. "So thick. What color, what life!" He settled Caitlin before a mirror and ran his hands through her wet hair. "We can do wonders with this!"

Caitlin watched his reflection warily. "It's always more or less had a mind of its own," she said. "I haven't had much luck with anything but a very simple cut. Please don't take too much off."

Jacques picked up the scissors with decision. "Ah, we must give your hair a chance to express itself without letting it run—what is the amusing expression—hog wild! Lift your head, please."

"I definitely don't want to look like a hog," Caitlin told him. "Look, uh, Jacques, I'm a very conservative person. And I hate to fuss with my hair, so if you could please restrain your creativity—"

Caitlin peeked up from under the dampened strands he had combed over her face. Jacques was holding the scissors at a threatening angle, and his expression was unreadable. Remembering the poster, she wondered if she had the courage to bolt, when he suddenly began to laugh.

"Okay," he said, his accent now unquestionably middle seaboard, "how about something medium length, just your natural curl, finger-dried under the heat lamp? No perms, no gels, no mousses. Trust me?"

Caitlin relaxed. "Yes, thank you. Do you have to baby nervous clients very often?"

Jacques snipped quickly but without losing concentration as he told a series of libelous stories about prominent local women whose hair he fashioned. He entertained her so well she was almost unaware of the number of shining locks dropping to the floor. Apprehension woke again while he arranged the lamp to his satisfaction, but she reminded herself that the worst had already been done and sat docilely when he returned to twist tendrils this way and that under the heat. Once back in front of the mirror, she gasped in pleasure.

Jacques had kept his word. Her hair was only slightly shorter than before. But he'd shingled it to release the soft curl and completely reshaped the top and sides to emphasize the contours of her face, with its broad, thoughtful brow, and to highlight her wide-set eyes. It curled sweetly, not conforming exactly to any standard cut, but tailored to suit her. He pulled it back and forward to demonstrate different effects. Caitlin was extravagant with her praise.

Jacques shrugged modestly. "It is only to release what is already there, hidden, until I come to remove the excess," he said in his campy French accent.

Caitlin said happily, "I think Michelangelo said that first, or words to that effect, but I thank you anyway. Will you accept a tip?"

Jacques looked pained. "Gratuity sounds so much nicer, don't you think?"

She agreed and left an extravagant sum. Her head felt lighter; she could feel the tendrils crisping at the base of her neck as she went in search of Auretta.

For an instant she hardly recognized the face under the absurd cap, her friend had been so plucked and plumped and bedizened with cosmetics. Auretta fluttered bright blue eyelashes half an inch long.

"What do you think?"

"I'm speechless."

"Coward. I bought a whole box of these wonderful lashes. I'm going to wear them to work. You look downright pretty. Let's see the back. *Yes*. You have emerged, Caitlin Stewart. Didn't I say that squirt would do you proud? Now you've got a chance with a real chunk of man like—"

"I am not doing all this to impress Lee Michaels," Caitlin said in a louder voice than she'd intended. She drew amused glances from all over the beauty salon and banged her way out the door, irritated with herself. Damn, damn, damn the man! He didn't even have to be nearby to make her flustered.

"Of course not," agreed Auretta. "Why would you want to impress the handsomest, sexiest, most eligible male on campus?"

4

CAITLIN ALLOWED HERSELF a lazy Sunday, playing with Flame and glancing through some professional journals. Toward late afternoon, she inspected her closetful of new clothes and finally decided on what her mother might have called a cocktail dress of shimmering green bronze. It was more sophisticated than anything she'd ever owned before and Caitlin experimented with her new haircut to do it justice. By sweeping it up at the sides she achieved a suitably polished look. Light touches of mascara, blusher and lipstick bolstered her morale enough to take her downstairs to pirouette for Toby.

He gaped.

"Too much?" she asked, more nervous than she had reason to be. After all, it wasn't as if anyone special was going to be at the Mallorys' sure-to-be-boring dinner party. Caitlin carefully refrained from defining *anyone special* even in her mind. "I mean, if I look ridiculous—"

"You look great," Toby assured her. "I've never seen you look so—I mean, usually you're just sort of—but this! It's—maybe I just better shut up, huh?"

Caitlin was regarding him with her hands on her satin-clad hips.

"Maybe you had. Okay, joking aside—assuming you were joking—am I really all right? Not too out of character?"

"Ma, you look terrific. Have fun at your party."

Caitlin picked up the small brocade purse she saved for going out. "I feel like I'm on my way to the prom."

Once she was admitted to the Mallorys' expensively nondescript living room, however, she saw she wasn't overdressed. The men were all in conservative suits, but the women either sparkled with sequins or frothed with lace. There were ten couples, she realized with surprise. With a smile for those she knew—all football fanatics, she noted, refusing to let the smile slip—Caitlin made her way to the kitchen, where she found Susanna Mallory removing a tray from under the broiler.

"What can I do to help?" she asked.

Susanna looked startled. Didn't anybody ever come back to give her a hand? Caitlin wondered. Then she noticed another woman, obviously hired help, and felt embarrassed.

"Nothing! That is, Ed wants you out there. I mean—what am I talking about? Hello, Caitlin, don't you look lovely." Susanna seemed limp in something black and depressing. "I know Ed was hoping to introduce you around. If you'll just take this tray to the rumpus room. Be careful, don't spoil that exquisite dress. Is it new...?"

Caitlin was eased out the swinging door. Susanna was always an anxiety-prone hostess, Caitlin remembered, and tonight she was acting more rattled than Caitlin had ever seen her. Her food was perfect, however, and the tray Caitlin passed among the people in the basement recreation area quickly emptied. She was returning it to the kitchen when Ed Mallory spied her and came rushing over.

"Now, now," he huffed, taking the tray from her hands, "what's Susanna thinking of, letting you wait on the other guests?"

"I wanted to help," Caitlin said quickly. Somehow she imagined Ed was capable of chastising his wife in public.

"Nonsense! You come on over here. There's somebody I want you to meet."

Beaming, he led her to a man whose big shoulders were encased in an immaculate sport coat. Caitlin felt Susanna's canapés settle leadenly to the bottom of her stomach.

Lee was speaking to someone Caitlin couldn't see. He turned with reluctance and said, "Hello, Caitlin."

"Hi," she answered with the same lack of enthusiasm.

"Well, well," said Ed. "I see you two have already met." He seemed to realize then that he still held the empty tray. He flourished it with a weak grin and disappeared in the direction of the kitchen.

"Caitlin," Lee said in a neutral tone, "this is Tamara. Tamara, Caitlin."

Lee moved slightly, so the person behind him became visible. Caitlin's eyes widened. The blonde standing there was breathtakingly tall, with the leggy perfection that invited comparisons to long-stemmed roses. Her gown—it couldn't be called a dress—was a white chiffon calculated to set off an even tan. Its measured folds were vaguely Greek and did nothing to disguise her upstanding breasts and well-exercised waistline.

Caitlin instantly felt short and consequently insignificant. This was the kind of young woman one usually saw striding in killer high heels up and down a runway under the glare of television lights, not in a neighbor's rumpus room. Caitlin wasn't inspired with any sense of rivalry. Her main desire was to go someplace and hide.

There was an awkward silence that even Lee with his glib tongue didn't try to bridge. Years ago, he might have flaunted someone like Tamara in front of someone like Caitlin, hoping for a reaction. Now he merely felt weary distaste for such an adolescent tactic.

After the disastrous ending to Friday night's confrontation, he'd told himself to get his hormones under better control and had half convinced himself he'd been successful. At least he'd spent the weekend immersed in work. Although his too gregarious host had confided that Coach Stewart's widow was invited to this party, Lee had been able to regard the get-together with indifference.

He'd forced himself to come because the guest roster was filled with football supporters, making the gathering an extension of his investigation, but he'd expected to be bored and he had been . . . until Caitlin appeared, towed along by Ed Mallory, who suddenly didn't seem like such a bad fellow after all.

She was looking both startled and sullen as she glanced up from under her lashes, first at him, then at Tamara. Lee surveyed the room, trying to locate Tamara's date. The blonde had detached herself from her escort and attached herself to him the moment she'd spotted him. A complete stranger, she was a type he recognized all too well.

A barracuda.

The signs were unmistakable. The provocative smile, the calculating eyes and the single-minded tenacity all belonged to a female predator who'd never suffered a rebuff. Lee had no doubt she'd be willing to ditch her erstwhile boyfriend, and the only emotion she inspired in him was disgust. As a naive rookie, new to the pros, he, too, had played the game of predator and prey, until the day he'd overheard two of his transient lovers comparing notes on his performance in bed and realized that he'd been the prey all along. The lesson had provided a humiliating but swift cure. He had no more respect for the women who stalked him than he had for himself; after all, that younger Lee had thought he was the one taking advantage, getting something when he had no intention of giving anything, stealing pleasure as if love had no price tag. He reflected he was damned lucky that none of the experience he'd gained had been accompanied by anything communicable.

At least he'd learned enough to value a Caitlin when she suddenly, miraculously, materialized in his life.

The reluctant object of his unruly desires, every diminutive inch of her, adorable in something green and rustling that reminded Lee irresistibly of his older sister's prom dress, looked as unobtainable as ever. In fact, he would have bet the contents of his wallet she was ready to bolt. There was an edgy quality to her silence.

Even though it was obvious she was still stubbornly refusing to acknowledge the attraction that flared between them, Lee felt almost light-headed with optimism. What would she do, he wondered, if he threw caution overboard and simply grabbed her, à la John Wayne, for a long, deep kiss that would claim her for his own in front of all these nice, dull, respectable people?

A realistic assessment of Caitlin's temper suggested that she was quite capable of slapping him, very, very hard, across the face. Or beaning him with an ashtray. Or dousing his ardor with a drink. But remembering the way she'd felt in his arms—yielding, fervent, sweetly vulnerable—he decided it would be worth it.

He made a quick, abortive movement toward her just as she murmured something about meeting someone upstairs and fled.

As Caitlin practically ran up the carpeted stairs, she heard Tamara say, "Who's she?" in a dismissive way. Lee didn't say anything at all.

To her amazement the evening was destined to get worse, after Susanna, who was looking exhausted, directed guests to prearranged seats at little tables scattered throughout the dining and living areas. Caitlin found the place-card with her name on it at a piecrust table in a corner just as Lee sat in the chair next to hers.

He shot her the flicker of a smile. "We seem to be dinner partners. How are you, Caitlin?"

"Fine, thanks."

She was annoyed that her voice sounded breathless. It was ridiculous, she thought, that the most banal exchange between them was charged with sexual tension.

"You changed your hair."

Her hand flew up to the clips. They hadn't slipped, thank goodness.

"Yes, it seemed—to be time for a change."

"I like it. What's it like when you let it down?" Lee asked conversationally.

Caitlin gasped as if he'd said something very personal. It was impossible to tell if he'd meant the remark the way it sounded in his deep, caressing voice. Before she could think of an answer, a shadow fell between them.

"Here you are, Lee. Do you know, these brainless people put me way on the other side of the room? We'll fix that. Here, take this—"

Tamara calmly began transferring a place setting from the nearest table to theirs. With supreme self-confidence, she distributed the setting in the small space between Caitlin and Lee and pulled a chair over to sink gracefully into it.

Lee's face was a polite mask, but as Caitlin's eyes, huge with astonishment, met his, she saw they were glinting dangerously. For an instant, something flared in the air, then Caitlin looked firmly down at her intertwined fingers. A balloon of laughter filled her chest, but she couldn't very well laugh in Tamara's face, or rather, at her back, for a slight twist of bare shoulders put Caitlin on the outside of a circle that enclosed only Tamara and Lee.

Resisting the impulse to peer around the blond hair that was spiked in such careful disorder, Caitlin applied herself to the food, which deserved respectful attention. Salmon mousse, roast lamb decorated with mint and new potatoes were followed by an architecturally perfect almond torte. From the appearance of Lee's dishes as they were removed, Caitlin concluded that he, too, was appreciating the dinner, but Tamara ate almost nothing. Instead she talked.

With no discernible effort, she filled the silence with a soft babble that centered on Tamara: her tennis game, her aerobics class, the car she wanted to buy, the car her daddy had bought for her instead, the selfishness of fathers, the polish on her fingernails. It was hard to believe that so much shallowness had been allowed to survive undisturbed by the school system or parental influence for twenty or twenty-one years. Even when the guests moved to the bar for liqueurs, Tamara's breathy, insistent flow of words continued to trap Lee at her side. Now she was confiding to him the ratio of cocoa butter to glycerin in her tanning oil.

Caitlin sat still for a while. She'd refused wine with dinner and didn't want to spoil the memory of that torte with a sweet, heavy drink. If she waited a minute or two for appearance's sake, perhaps the Mallorys wouldn't take offense at her leaving early.

She definitely intended to leave early.

Caitlin had just decided to risk her exit when Lee sat beside her with a cup and saucer in each hand. "Thought you could use this."

"Oh! Thank you." Caitlin sipped coffee she didn't want but that tasted surprisingly good, and watched Lee arrange his long legs. "Where's the bombshell?"

That earned her a look. "Firmly deposited with the poor schmuck who brought her. You weren't much help."

"*Me?* How was I supposed to know you needed—or wanted—any help?"

Lee said softly, reproachfully, "Caitlin."

Trying to maintain a light tone, she continued, "After all, most guys would be thrilled just to look at a girl like that."

"As long as they could disconnect the sound," Lee agreed.

Caitlin made an indignant little noise. "Oh, come on. For that body to come equipped with brains would require an imbalance of nature. Besides, you can't expect me to believe that somebody like—that ninety-nine guys out of a hundred would care if she makes intellectual conversation or not."

Lee set down his cup with a snap. "Say what you mean. You don't expect somebody like me to care about anything but what? Appearances? Sex? That's the sort of remark I'd anticipate from Tamara, because that's all she's interested in herself. But you? Just what do you think you know about me, Caitlin? Or is there nothing to know? Scratch my facade and you find a veneer?"

So shocked was Caitlin by his sudden, white-hot fury that she simply stared at him.

A muscle twitched in his cheek. "I see. That makes things very clear—again."

He seemed about to say or do something else, but he bit back whatever it was, stood with a jerk and strode away.

Caitlin sat feeling small, her breathing awry, before she slipped out of the room as unobtrusively as possible.

Her purse was in the kitchen, she remembered. At least she could make sure she didn't end another evening leaving it behind. The little rectangle was still resting on the counter where she'd dropped it. As she picked it up, Susanna drifted in, murmuring apologies.

"As if anyone could guess what she'd do, dreadful girl, but her father does business with Ed, so when she said she wanted to meet Lee Michaels..."

Caitlin repressed a scream. "Susanna, what are you talking about?"

"Tamara, of course. The way she barged over to your table and preempted the football star. You might be used to that, from before?" Susanna looked mildly inquiring.

With difficulty, Caitlin realized Susanna was referring to her marriage with Jim. "Well, no. Jim wasn't— and I don't recall ever encountering anything quite so direct before. But it's all right. It didn't matter," she said drearily.

"Didn't matter?" For the first time, Susanna showed animation. "She ruined my seating arrangement! One table was left with odd numbers. Two, counting yours. And what must Lee Michaels have thought! Ed wanted to make such a good impression. And Lee came back to the kitchen to ask specially for you to be his table mate. I switched the place-cards!" she declared so dramatically that Caitlin smiled. The amused curve of her lips faded as Susanna added, "It was so romantic. I mean, he's so handsome and you've got so much in common, football and all, and it's really convenient that you're, ah . . ."

"That I'm free?" Caitlin suggested. "That my husband is dead? Why, Susanna, you're the romantic. I never realized."

Caitlin didn't trust herself to say anything more. She turned abruptly and bumped through the swinging door, leaving Susanna in her drab dress staring after her.

5

"I NEED TO FIND OUT about microdensitometers." The student smiled at Caitlin hopefully.

"Okay, what do you need to know?"

"Anything. Everything."

Caitlin winced. This boy's approach didn't argue any special aptitude for studying microdensiwhatevers, or possibly anything else. "It sounds as if you want to cover the subject from the general to the specific." Caitlin gave him a brief lecture on how to use the library.

"Indians?" he repeated doubtfully.

Caitlin sighed. "Indices. Indexes. Plural of index." When he continued to look blank, she explained about indexes.

"Uh, well, I sort of figured that maybe you could, you know, do all that stuff and then tell me what you found out. You know."

She closed her eyes. Her head didn't ache exactly, but since the night two weeks ago when Lee Michaels had walked away from her, it seemed somehow to be more and more difficult to concentrate on the routine of everyday life. Like students who assumed librarians were homework machines.

Opening her eyes and shaking her head, Caitlin said, "Sorry. I'm not allowed to do that. You go ahead and give it a try. If it seems too complicated, come on back and I can refer you to the tutoring center." She said the last gently, noticing that the boy's mouth had developed a tragic droop.

He shambled off toward the exit, and Caitlin sighed again.

She loved her work. As an academic librarian, she generally dealt with bright people, with the same ingrained habits of quiet and industry she'd made part of herself. Her station in the reference section smelled faintly of the dry, old leather and new ink of the books that surrounded it. The books were supplemented by a clutter of technological reinforcements: computer keyboard and monitor, microfiche and microfilm readers. The squeaky chair and scarred desk top were completely familiar and completely comfortable.

Every now and then, though, she felt a twinge of dissatisfaction. She'd never know if that boy found out anything about microdensitometers, if he flunked out tomorrow or went on to become the microdensitometer expert of the world.

These first few weeks of the semester she'd run into more than the usual number of hapless students. She wondered if her perception of this year's crop of freshmen was colored by the fact she wasn't sleeping very well. In the daylight hours she could put Lee and his triple-damned investigation out of her mind—unless, of course, another one of Jim's old buddies called, "Just to let you know that conference guy's been asking a few questions." As far as she could tell, Lee must have interviewed everyone in town who'd ever known Jim, except maybe his first grade teacher.

But at night, when the walls she had built dissolved, Lee became a recurring character in the shadowy dramas that plagued her sleep. Waking before first light with her lips burning from the aftermath of his dream kisses, Caitlin found it less harrowing to rise after only four hours of rest and begin a new day than to lie in bed. The early-morning stillness was too conducive to thoughts about Lee and football and the increasingly gnawing reflection that she'd been waking up alone, and lonely, for three whole years now. Her eyes had developed a habit of staring off into the distance, and they always felt hot and dry. She didn't bother trying to hide the purplish shadows stamped in crescent-moon shapes underneath them.

She shook herself and glanced at her watch. Time for a break. As she was pulling her purse from the lockable drawer where she kept her personal items, the phone buzzed. Caitlin was tempted to pretend she hadn't heard it. With another sigh, she picked up the receiver. "Reference."

"Mrs. Stewart? This is Mrs. Watters, President Silverthorne's secretary. The president has appointed you to a committee that will be meeting in conference room B at three o'clock this afternoon. Will you be able to make it?"

Caitlin was startled. "Well, I'll have to arrange with the head librarian for a substitute—"

"Good," the secretary said, overriding Caitlin's objection. "I'll tell the president you accept."

"Wait!" Caitlin almost shrieked. Heads raised all over the room. "What committee is this? Who chairs it?"

There was an audible sniff. "The Oversight Committee for Compliance with Conference Regulations in Varsity Sports. Marvin Dendorf, Chair."

Caitlin heard a click and then the dial tone. Oh, hell. She gathered up her purse and walked to the elevator with brows drawn together. She knew Marvin Dendorf, an austere man whose only enthusiasm seemed to be breeding tropical fish. He'd told her all about the subject at a faculty tea once.

How had someone like that gotten himself entangled in varsity sports? More to the point, how was she going to get herself disentangled?

The committee, she dimly recalled, had been formed during the summer, right after the scandal broke, to monitor the football program. Perhaps Marvin's main qualification was disinterest. As far as she was aware, no one could accuse him of knowing the university had a football team, let alone of corrupting the players.

That left the question of her own last-minute appointment. Was a previous appointee now unable to serve? It would take a brave staff or faculty member to back out of a direct order from President Silverthorne. His teddy-bear paternalism was balanced by an iron code of responsibility he expected his subordinates to share. It was one of the qualities Caitlin especially liked about him. No shirking of the unpleasant things of life—like committee meetings—was allowed.

The head librarian was in his office, sprawled with his feet up reading the *Chronicle of Higher Education*. When he saw Caitlin at his door, he left his feet where they were.

He greeted her news with a ferocious scowl but grumblingly agreed to find someone to cover her desk. He recognized a command performance as well as she did.

There was no time for Caitlin to brood in the early afternoon, which brought a flood of students all looking for the same book. The only copy was missing. Caitlin made a hurried note to suggest that Auretta purchase duplicates. This was the second year the same teacher had assigned the title without requesting that the library and the bookstore stock sufficient copies for his class.

So it was in a doubly disgruntled mood that she stepped briskly into the wind blowing across campus. Annoyance, combined with the chill breeze, brightened her tired eyes and tore her hair into a riot of curls. Once she found the committee room, she concentrated on the chance to get warm, choosing a folding chair that fell under a dusty sunbeam from the one window.

Other chairs filled quickly. Besides Caitlin there were Marvin; Auretta's nonphysical physics professor, who turned out to be the faculty liaison with the football conference; somebody from English; somebody else from engineering; and a very nervous young secretary. Six people. Pads, pencils and a thick sheaf of papers detailing conference rules were laid neatly before seven chairs. Who—

Was there no escape? Caitlin asked herself when Lee walked in and settled himself across from her. He gave her one level glance before smiling at the others. The secretary wriggled like a lovelorn cocker spaniel.

Marvin ignored the pencil in front of him and produced a gold pen, which he used to tap for order. "Now that we're all here . . ."

Caitlin had to admit he accomplished the committee's parliamentary business with Teutonic dispatch. The secretary fell victim to the group's clerical chores.

Physics made a brief speech about TPU's many successes on the playing field. English made a much longer speech about experiences playing Little League baseball, circa 1960. Engineering doodled on his pad. The secretary took down every word in shorthand.

Caitlin looked everywhere except directly across the table, where Lee's devil eyes were waiting for her.

There was a lull.

Lee couldn't keep his attention from straying to Caitlin. The meeting was deadly. He didn't even know why his attendance had been requested. But the snippy woman on the telephone had been quite specific. The president wanted it, so the president got it.

While the group as a whole was as predictable and inane as any other committee he'd ever sat in on, Caitlin as always was unexpected. Whose bright idea was her presence, anyway? If there was one thing she'd made painfully clear, it was that she despised football. And ex-football players. And current football league officials.

Despite the physical distance between them he felt her tension. Had he not been in love with her, he thought, he might even have said she looked less than her best. Healthy color had rushed into her features when he entered, but it had quickly faded. The ivory pallor visible between her freckles, accompanied as it was by dark circles under her eyes, seemed to indicate that something was keeping her up nights.

He hoped he was the culprit, as she'd been costing him lost sleep and endless cold showers. It had taken him two days to strangle the bitter rage he'd carried to his motel room from the Mallorys' ill-fated dinner party, but at last common sense and an instinct to defend Caitlin even against himself had intervened.

What, after all, did she know about him? Just because he'd taken a serious header for her didn't mean she had to feel the same way. Desire was there, he knew, and loneliness. But those were the ingredients for a one-night stand, not the kind of long-term loving that automatically dominated his thoughts whenever they turned to Caitlin. And she pushed herself into his mind more and more frequently as the days, then weeks, passed.

She was more potent than a drug. After precisely three meetings and one—albeit very nice—kiss, he was obsessed with her.

Finally, it was almost a relief to admit to himself that he wasn't just infatuated with her, or exasperated by her or tempted by her luscious little bosom and slender legs and compact behind. He loved her. She was smart and funny, tart and sweet at the same time. She was everything he'd given up expecting to find. And from all the signs, she was still in love with a man who'd been dead for years.

For the first time in his life, Lee didn't know how to attract a woman.

In the meantime, he reminded himself now, there was work. Sensing a chance to make some converts—you never knew who might have useful information in an investigation like this, although this bunch, barring Caitlin, seemed like an unlikely bet—he leaned forward. "I hope it's all right if I jump in here to explain just what the conference is hoping to accomplish at Tall Pines."

He gave a brief résumé of the violations and the steps taken to assure that the guilty parties had no further ties to the university. "Naturally, the focus is on making sure nothing like this happens again. But we also feel an obligation—to the honest players, their parents, the fans, the other schools in the conference—to discover how far back the corruption goes and what employees of the university may have been involved."

Jim, thought Caitlin. He actually believes *Jim* could have been bribing players.

Engineering was talking. "How do you intend to get results?"

Lee shrugged. "Ask a few questions, check a few documents. Contrary to rumor, I don't use—I believe the suggestion was thumbscrews."

There was polite laughter.

The bland mockery in Lee's voice, audible only to her, prodded Caitlin into speech. "What about returning players compromised last year?" she asked.

All eyes swiveled to her, amused, accusing, uncomprehending. Caitlin set her chin and faced Lee a little defiantly.

He gave her a slow, easy smile. At least he'd gotten her to admit he was in the room. "Perhaps your faculty liaison is the best person to answer that. I'd like you to remember," he added with the slightest accent on *you*, "that this unfortunate situation was uncovered before I was called in."

The physics professor cleared his throat. "The university has been very anxious to put this unpleasant incident behind . . ."

The afternoon oozed away as he pontificated. Caitlin decided to tell Auretta she'd had a lucky escape. This old windbag would have bored her lively friend into catatonia.

Caitlin's sunbeam crept across the table to light the back of Lee's hand. It glinted on the metal band at the end of his pencil and gilded the minute lines that crisscrossed his olive skin. He had elegant, tapering fingers. Really, Caitlin thought, if it weren't for the strong column of his neck and the bulk of muscle in his shoulders and thighs, he might be taken for a poet as easily as a quarterback.

"So, in conclusion . . ."

Caitlin wrenched her attention back to the speaker, who finally ran down. Interested in spite of herself, Caitlin asked, "How many freshmen recruited for the team have actually shown up this semester?"

The other committee members looked blank. With a sigh, Lee answered, "Almost all. Only four were no-shows. To be a little more honest than your coaches might like, they were the most promising new players TPU had signed. I can't say they had any trouble finding schools willing to admit them at the last minute."

He sounded so wry that Caitlin was startled until it struck her with a fresh jolt that his job was to be suspicious. Of everything and everyone who had anything to do with college football. She dragged up knowledge she'd thought she'd forgotten and said, "In other words, Tall Pines is facing a season with half the returning players disqualified and the new recruits decimated."

For a lady who professed to know nothing and care even less about the game of football, thought Lee, Caitlin was certainly shining in comparison to the rest of the members of the Oversight Committee.

Once again, his smile was just for her. Something melted in the pit of Caitlin's stomach.

"I don't think things are quite that bad. Perhaps you would like to see the team practice. It just so happens," he said innocently, "I'm going to the practice tomorrow myself. I know any member of this committee would be welcome as well. You'd get a better idea of the players' caliber and the attitude of your coaches."

He hesitated, then said seriously, "People tend to think of the conference as an officious busybody, trying to force colleges into impossible standards of conduct. That's not true. The amateur ideal—playing for the sheer love of it—is an achievable goal. The most important thing any athlete can take from his or her competition is a sense of the joy of sport. That's what football gave to me and I'm hoping that when I'm finished with my job here, it's what TPU's players get, too."

The secretary sighed. Caitlin was aware of several smug looks cast in her direction. Lee was definitely the victor in their verbal contest, and she hadn't even meant to start a fight. A familiar swell of indignation filled her chest.

His gaze was so steady she couldn't look away. Her heart began the ridiculous staccato beat it always seemed to pick up around Lee.

He said, "Practice is at three-thirty. Come out tomorrow and take a look. I'm sure you know where the field is."

It was a deliberate challenge, and Caitlin gasped. The others were all watching with interest. She swallowed and said, "I'll see if I can get away. I have the eight to five shift tomorrow."

Accepting this ungracious response coolly, Lee said, "Good. I'll look forward to seeing you."

The group broke up. Lee strode out first. Caitlin followed, after taking a minute to help the secretary collect her notes. Clutching binder, purse and papers, the woman exhaled one last heartfelt sigh.

"Wow. He's cu-u-ute."

6

THE NEXT DAY'S RAINFALL washed away the golden autumn haze and replaced it with a muzzy drizzle that dogged Caitlin even inside the artificially lit, temperature-controlled stacks of the library. Auretta commiserated with her over the weather at lunch, but brightened as soon as she heard Caitlin's destination later in the day.

"Not really? The practices have been closed! I don't suppose you could sneak one teensy-weensy interloper in with you? I'd love to watch."

Caitlin started to shake her head but paused. After all, why not? She was a bona fide member of the Oversight Committee, dragooned against her will into attending a stupid, sweaty football practice. Somebody might as well come along and have a good time.

"Sure. You won't get into trouble for leaving your desk?"

"Honey, I've got enough leave time to take a world cruise."

The precipitation had decreased to a heavy mist by the time they sat side by side with their knees drawn up, watching a horde of teenagers squelch back and forth across the soggy field. Caitlin shifted her bottom. She must have blocked out memories of the extremely hard, cold aluminum bleachers. Auretta seemed perfectly happy on the plastic air cushion emblazoned with the Tall Pines seal she'd brought with her.

"Wherever did you find that thing?" Caitlin asked her.

"The university bookstore, of course."

"Of course. You can't find any books in the bookstore, but stuff like that—by the way, I need to write you a memo."

For a few minutes, they talked books and publishers and professors, but Auretta was too enthralled with the preview of the team to discuss anything else for long.

"Will you look at that? Bad hands, bad hands. Do you think he knows he's running the wrong way? Oops, well, there goes a rib, at least."

Caitlin wrapped her coat closer. The dense, chill air had a way of penetrating straight to the skin.

A number of men in identical windbreakers stood at the sidelines, eyelids puckered, occasionally calling out words smothered by the mist. Most had their hoods pulled up. It was odd how Caitlin was able to pick Lee out from the group immediately and, even though she was careful to turn her attention elsewhere, how often she was aware of him. His hood was down. Water had made his hair a black cap that hugged the subtle shape of his head.

"I don't know what he's doing here at practice, anyway," Caitlin said suddenly, without bothering to identify *him*. "He's just an outsider, really. A paid snoop."

Auretta chuckled. "Look at them. You can't blame the coaches for wanting his advice. After all, he was a pro. And let's face it, it's a good thing the head coach is retiring after this year. You don't think our beloved president was going to keep him around as a reminder of Tall Pines' darkest hour, do you? He was just an interim replacement after Jim—till they could find somebody really capable of the job. Lee Michaels, now," she said, gesturing. "Do you wonder the staff want his help?"

Here in his chosen place, Lee seemed to emit energy even when he stood completely still. Caitlin had the thought that Lee was the motor, the driving piston that kept all the others on the field in motion. Without him all this movement would lose its underlying purpose and drift to a stop.

"No," she admitted with a sigh. "I suppose it's only natural."

Lee didn't do anything to make Caitlin think he'd noticed their presence, but at the end of the practice, as the muddy players trailed into the field house, he was waiting at the bottom of the metal stairs.

"What do you think?" he asked.

Caitlin huddled deeper into her coat, and after a moment, Auretta burst into praise so lavish Caitlin's jaw dropped.

Lee said, "Well, I'll pass on your kind words, but frankly, I'd say the team's got a lot of work to put in before their first game. Unfortunately it's tonight."

Auretta didn't even blush. "All right, maybe these boys aren't ready for the Super Bowl yet, but I can see the makings of a fine team there."

Lee grinned. "Right now the coaches are emphasizing the basics and keeping their fingers crossed. Did you notice anything in particular, Caitlin?"

She said, "I'm not very knowledgeable. Everybody seemed to be working hard."

"No words of wisdom from the Oversight Committee?"

"The purpose of that committee is not to oversee play, as you knew full well when you maneuvered me into coming out here this afternoon, Lee Michaels. I will be able to tell my colleagues there were no dancing girls, gallon jars of drugs or expensive convertibles distributed in my presence, if that'll make you happy."

Instantly his mouth became grave. "I'm sure the coaching staff will thank you." He glanced at his watch. "They asked me to join them for their strategy session, so—"

"Don't you go worrying your head about us, now, we'll be just fine," Auretta called as Lee caught up with one of the assistant coaches. She turned on Caitlin and hissed, "What's the matter with you?"

"With me? What was all that stuff about the Super Bowl? You didn't seem very impressed with the players during the practice!"

"Well, I couldn't tell him that, not with him begging you for one single syllable of interest. Which, I might say, you were too stingy to give him."

That surprised an angry laugh from Caitlin. "Don't tell me you think that man is languishing for approval from me!"

"Didn't he invite you specially to this practice?" Auretta demanded. "Can't you tell when a man wants to impress you?"

"Wait a minute! How do you know he invited me?"

Auretta smiled a secret smile. "You're not the only person I know on that committee."

"Not the human icicle from physics! Oh, Auretta, I'm sorry. I shouldn't have said that." Caitlin was appalled at herself.

"It's all right, honey. You're under a strain," said Auretta magnanimously. "Besides, I've. said worse myself. He's got some good points and I'm working on bringing them out. But you've distracted me. The subject is that adorable Lee Michaels."

"He's—he's—"

"Yes? He's what?" Auretta asked.

Caitlin shrugged irritably and searched the skyline of the campus for clues. Auretta was looking stern. She wasn't going to be put off by evasions. Caitlin wasn't really good at subterfuge. If something was important enough to lie about, then it was important enough for the truth. And she was uncomfortably aware that Lee, in the few weeks since she'd met him, had become important.

Slowly she said, "He's all the things you keep saying he is. Good-looking, available, eligible—and sexy. Very sexy. He makes me . . . I haven't felt this way since . . . I really would like to have something with him."

The wind tore the words from her lips, but she heard them echo in her brain. They sounded wistful. Adjectives for something—someone—decidedly desirable but beyond her reach.

"But?"

Caitlin shrugged. "But?"

Auretta said impatiently, "There was a 'but' in there someplace. I heard it distinctly."

"But, well, it's just not right for me. Or him, probably. He deserves more than I could give him. And I'm happy with my life. I've got Toby, a house that's paid for, a good job, *security*. There's nothing in the way I live that's out of place or out of sync. I'm happy."

Auretta poked her. "I'll tell you what you are and that's abnormal. You never go anyplace or do anything. That house of yours is like a museum. Why don't you date? You have no friends your own age. No young thing like you should be hanging around with an old crock like me! And," she finished triumphantly, "you cuddle up to a cat at night when there's an absolutely fascinating man who—who stands up like an exclamation point every time you come into view." Auretta stopped herself and then continued, "However, it's your business and I suppose you know it best. I'm going to check in my office for messages. You coming with me?"

Auretta's spurt of righteous anger seemed to be over. Caitlin smiled and shook her damp curls. "I have to think of something to do with a pound of hamburger. Toby's probably bringing a friend home for dinner."

"Sounds exciting," said Auretta scathingly. "When that stepson of yours makes you a grandmother at thirty and you decline into a permanent weekend babysitter, don't say I didn't warn you."

"No, I won't be able to say that, will I?" Caitlin chuckled, and gave Auretta a hug. The woman meant well, she thought.

When she got home she found a scribbled note from Toby that Brenda's mother was providing him with supper. Caitlin grimaced as she weighed the dripping package of hamburger in her hand. "So what do you think, Flame?" she asked the cat, who was delicately licking the drops falling to the floor.

Flame was too busy to answer, so Caitlin placed a bit of ground meat in her dish and set it in front of the red-

dened nose. Apparently the drips had been enough, for
Flame ignored the tidbit and swarmed up a stool to sit
with her tail wrapped around her legs in Egyptian maj-
esty.

"You know, that's what I think, too," said Caitlin
with sudden vigor. The hamburger was thrust back into
the meat compartment while she peered into the depths
of the refrigerator. There was nothing inside that
looked outstandingly edible or matched her mood. She
abandoned the perishables and wandered into the old-
fashioned pantry to survey the contents of the "mad"
shelf. This was where she and Toby kept their crazier
impulse purchases, things that they later decided they
didn't want or considered too expensive to bring out
except for holidays or guests.

It might not be a special occasion, but that was no
reason, Caitlin told herself, to eat meatloaf. As a matter of fact, she made an excellent meatloaf. But it was
hardly luxurious and she'd had a hard day. Surely it was
permissible for her to coddle herself a little tonight.

Flame seemed to agree, because she jumped onto the
shelf and nosed out a small can Caitlin had forgotten
was there.

"What's this? Caviar! Good heavens. What else is
back there?"

Further search revealed an even smaller can containing one imported truffle. That reminded her there was
a porterhouse steak hiding in the freezer.

A short while later, Caitlin and Flame were nibbling
black roe—Caitlin's on buttery toast points, Flame's à
la carte—as Caitlin gauged the temperature under her
reliable cast-iron skillet. Too much heat and the still-
rigid slab of beef would be charcoal on the outside and

crystalline on the inside. Not enough and it would be warmed to an unpalatable tan clear through. The last bit of caviar rolled and burst on her tongue in a tiny explosion of salty flavor. Now or never. She tipped the meat into the pan.

The steak was wonderful. She was justly proud of the sauce to go with it that she concocted from the truffle, and politely declined to share any with Flame. The cat didn't express much interest in the salad, though, so Caitlin was allowed to finish the simple wedge of lettuce in peace.

When the last bite was finished, she savored a moment of pure satiation before rising to clear the table.

"Ma! Hey, Ma!"

Doors crashed and oversize feet pounded into the kitchen. Flame melted away.

"Ma, you'll never guess what!" Toby was radiant.

"What, what?" Caitlin asked, laughing. "Hi, Brenda."

"Hi, Mrs. Stewart." Brenda was blond with owlish glasses that hid neither her gamine prettiness nor her alert brown eyes. This evening a rosy flush rode delicately in her cheeks, and the wary look she usually showed in Caitlin's presence had been replaced by one of pure glee.

"Have you eaten? Sit. Talk," Caitlin ordered.

"Yeah, we ate—not what you had, though, huh, Brenda?" Toby said, regarding the wreckage of Caitlin's meal. "We had meatloaf. It was good," he added hastily.

Brenda said, "Well, go on, tell her. Silly."

"Okay. Sheesh. I was over at the gym to pick up Brenda after her fencing class and just sort of, you know, hanging around."

"Uh-huh," said Caitlin encouragingly.

"Then this really sharp guy comes out of one of the offices and sort of does a double take when he sees me. Of course, I knew who he was right away—"

Caitlin stiffened.

"But how he recognized me, I don't know. Anyway, you'll never guess who it was! Go on, give it a try." Toby beamed at Caitlin.

Woodenly she said, "I couldn't possibly."

"It was Lee Michaels! You know, he used to play for—"

"I know."

"Oh. Anyhow, he wanted to talk to me. We got cans out of the pop machine and sat on the floor of the gym and he told me all about the pros."

Caitlin kept her voice calm. "And what else?"

Toby looked puzzled. "There wasn't any 'what else.' Except that he said he'd be winding up his investigation pretty soon."

Relief seeped through Caitlin. He was going away. Her life could resume its even, stressless pace. She'd probably survive to a hundred years, without the strain that being near him put on her treacherous heartbeat. But why did relief feel so much like a stomachache?

Brenda took up the tale. "That's about the time I came out of the showers. Toby was telling him—"

In response to Brenda's nudge, Toby grinned and continued. "I was telling him that Dad used to keep some of his professional papers out at the cabin—"

"And did he need any of them to check anything—"

"And Brenda's folks invited me to the lake next weekend with them—"

"And we'd be perfectly glad to ferry him over to your summer place—"

"Because, let's face it, our boat is permanently out of commission—"

"Yes, I know that," Caitlin interrupted at last. "I was the one the marine patrol towed when the engine pooped out. Let me get this straight. Lee Michaels wants those old files your father used to keep at our cabin?"

"Well, yeah, sure," Toby said. "From what he was saying, he's read every piece of paper produced by the athletic department since the school was founded. He's thorough."

Caitlin looked from one young, eager face to the other. "Toby, doesn't it *bother* you, what Lee's doing?"

He spread his hands. Like his feet, they were overgrown. "Yeah, it bothers me. A lot. In fact, I hate it." He seemed to pick his words with great care. "Lee Michaels is a pretty impressive guy. I don't think he'd ask me things that'd put me in a bind to answer. And he won't find out anything that's not there. He's only doing his job. An important job."

There was something odd about Toby's turn of phrase, but Caitlin couldn't put her finger on what it was. "I agree, but—okay, so you told him he could have access to Jim's private files."

"It can't do any harm," Toby said quickly. "I went through that old stuff a long time ago. There's nothing damaging in it."

"Naturally there's nothing damaging in it," she replied, but absently. "The point is, Lee—that is, Mr.

Michaels—doesn't have to traipse all the way out to the lake." *Over my dead body,* she was thinking.

"Mrs. Stewart—"

"Brenda, I was going to rent a little speedboat and go close the cabin for the winter anyway." She considered. "I can box up those old records and cart them back to town if he's absolutely got to see them."

"But there's no need, Mrs. Stewart," said Brenda urgently. "My family's going to be at the lake anyway. Really, it's all set—you don't have to do a thing. Well, not much of anything," she added.

"Right," said Caitlin with suspicion. "Maybe you'd better spell out what my limited duties would be according to this scenario."

"Practically nothing," Toby assured her.

Brenda explained earnestly, "You see, my father's kind of juvenile. And he'd kill to be able to boast that a real pro football player rode around in his boat."

"And I suppose it's just barely possible you already talked this over with Mr. Michaels," Caitlin said to the ceiling.

The silence was a sufficient answer.

After a minute, Toby continued cautiously, "Not only that, but Lee had this great idea. He thought if we all—you and me and Lee and Brenda—if we started off with Brenda's parents on the long weekend they're planning, that they wouldn't mind if Brenda spent Friday night with us at our cabin. So the only thing you have to do is agree to be our chaperon."

Caitlin didn't know whether to laugh or cry. Auretta would have a fit. "You've got a class on Fridays."

"Beginning computer science. I can do that stuff in my sleep."

"I just don't think it's a very good idea," Caitlin said weakly. Toby looked so blasted happy about this hideous notion.

"It's only one day and night," Toby coaxed. "Brenda can give you a lift back to the marina anytime Saturday. Her dad practically said he'd give us the boat if he got to meet Lee. We need you to avoid the appearance of impropriety, Lee said."

"Appearances don't bother me. What am I supposed to do if I see any actual impropriety?"

"Ma!" Toby didn't quite succeed at sounding shocked.

"Mrs. Stewart!" Brenda's lenses magnified her eyes until they looked like saucers.

"I beg your pardon," Caitlin murmured. "I can tell such a thing never occurred to either of you."

"It's very uncool to do anything like that when parents are around," Brenda explained simply.

"And I'd only miss one class," Toby added.

"Has it dawned on you I have a job?"

"Ma, be honest. You've got vacation time coming out your ears."

This weekend jaunt sounded like a disaster in the making to Caitlin, but it was true that her unused vacation time was assuming ludicrous proportions. She remembered the note from personnel.

"Oh, all right. But only because the personnel director cries whenever he sees me. You've got a chaperon."

Brenda nodded in a satisfied way. Toby picked up Caitlin and swung her until she was dizzy, whooping the whole time. Finally Caitlin pounded on his arms with small, determined fists until he set her down, still gasping and grinning.

"Oh, Ma, Ma, I love you!"

"I love you, too, lummox," Caitlin said softly and peeked apologetically at Brenda. Toby's girlfriend was remarkably levelheaded, but no one could expect an eighteen-year-old to appreciate declarations of affection from her boyfriend to his unreasonably young stepmother.

Sure enough, Brenda became very prim and soon urged Toby to find his jacket. "We've got—"

"Oh. Oh, yeah. We've got someplace to go, Ma." For some reason, a little of the shining look faded from his open, ingenuous face. He said awkwardly, "You going to be okay?"

"Of course," said Caitlin. "Now, out!"

She walked them to the door. As they passed through the living room, Brenda said, "You know, I wonder how Lee Michaels knew Toby by sight. I guess he must have seen a picture of him somewhere, huh?" Her eyes moved thoughtfully to the snapshot of Toby in his cap and gown.

Caitlin remembered Lee studying that very photograph, and gritted her teeth. She'd provided him with the opportunity to memorize Toby's features the night she'd let him kiss her.

7

THE LATCH CLICKED quietly behind Toby and Brenda as sheer elemental fury overcame Caitlin. After a particularly inventive swearword, she stomped through the house looking for something to break. Her small whirlwind of destruction ended back in the kitchen, where she lashed out with a vindictive kick at Flame's bowl.

It was still spinning across the floor when Caitlin realized what she had done. Her frantic scramble failed to catch the blue blur before it crashed into a table leg and clattered to a stop.

She gasped with relief as she picked up the deceptively fragile-looking porcelain with trembling fingers. A tiny notch dented its circumference but the bowl was miraculously unshattered.

"Bless you, Mr. Wedgwood," she whispered.

A determined search revealed the transparent sliver that had broken off. It had boomeranged across the room to lie beneath the overhang of a low-set cupboard. Caitlin leaned against the knotty pine for a moment before she gathered her control and went to look for the glue.

A minute's finicky work had Toby's gift whole again. Caitlin ran her eyes over the rim to assure herself the repair was nearly invisible and placed the bowl carefully on the drainboard to dry. Stepping back, she rubbed her hands on her thighs to expel some of the tension that gripped her.

It was no use. She was still so spitting mad she could feel electricity coursing through her veins, sparking along her nerve endings. If she didn't find an outlet for all this static energy she'd short out.

A tentative purr distracted her. Flame had reappeared and was pawing her ankle for attention. Caitlin bent down, but Flame's built-in sensors apparently detected her unsettled emotions and the cat twisted away. A leap brought her up to her dish on the drainboard. She meowed piteously at the unfamiliar odor of glue, staring at Caitlin with narrowed amber eyes.

"Stop being such a piggy feline. You already had dinner," Caitlin scolded, but she shook some dry food onto a paper plate anyway and set it at Flame's accustomed place. Flame grumbled for a minute and then jumped down to crunch her dessert.

"Damn," said Caitlin, but Flame merely gave her an ironic look before focusing on her food once more.

It was obvious Flame wasn't going to be either comfort or company tonight. Caitlin's beloved house was actually stifling her with its walls and understated loveliness. The trouble was there wasn't anyplace else she particularly wanted to go.

She suddenly remembered the university pool. It was open nights.

In fifteen minutes she was shouldering open the big glass doors of the phys-ed center. Light and heat rushed out, drawing her in.

She sniffed. The building had been remodeled recently, but already it had accumulated that odd smell of humidity and sweat socks. A bored student waved her through the security gate without glancing at her ID.

The place was almost empty. Caitlin thought with an inner shrug that most people had something better to do with their Friday nights. She changed, showered and flipped her towel over her shoulder as she padded barefoot into the cavernous pool area.

One other person was there, a determined lap swimmer whose fast crawl sliced a glittering path through the water across the width at the deep end. Caitlin paused to admire his technique, the clean and simple way he used the force of his encounter with the upward curving side of the pool to push his body into a waterborne roll back onto course for the next lap. There was no wasted effort, just an impression of smooth, compelling power.

Caitlin dropped her towel and launched herself into a shallow dive from the side. Emulating the other swimmer, she did five laps to work off some of her excess ire before relaxing into a sidestroke. She liked being able to see where she was going, and wanted to stay well away from the expert, who was righting himself to tread water about twelve feet away. Conversation wasn't what she was looking for.

Turning to face the opposite direction, Caitlin paddled lazily, watching the tiny waves twinkle and dance under the fluorescent lights.

She hadn't swum much during the past summer, and when she had, she'd preferred the quiet of the lake near the family's semiprivate stretch of beach. After the outboard motor had conked out—for the last time, both Toby and the repair shop assured her—she'd tried this facility precisely once. The pool had literally been flooded with the rambunctious offspring of faculty. They'd churned the water with their dunkings and splashings and split the air with sixteen radios, all tuned to different stations. She hadn't been back till tonight.

Much as she was enjoying the swim, Caitlin wasn't strong in the water and exhaustion was starting to weigh her down. She caught hold of the bars set at the midway point just as her fellow swimmer heaved himself onto the concrete rim.

Caitlin's head naturally turned at the movement. Lee, streaming water, the muscles of his chest tensing into taut ridges, stared back at her. It should have been gratifying to discover she'd been right about his build; he was elegantly proportioned.

"You?" she said despairingly and remembered, too late, that he'd told her he swam every night.

An overwhelming sense of inevitability numbed Caitlin. Her grip on the slippery metal shifted, slipped and sent her crashing backward into the pool. Stunned, she felt her arms and legs flounder, but the motion only carried her farther down. She gulped water. It stung her nose, her eyes, her lungs. The bottom bumped into her. Panicked, she couldn't summon the necessary control to propel herself back to the top. Despite her best intentions, her aching lungs sucked in another few ounces of chlorinated water.

I cannot drown in five feet of water, she thought. But even as the words formed in her mind, she knew that plenty of people had.

Another body was with hers in the hot, raw blackness. An arm of steel circled her chest. A fist with the strength of shackles grabbed and held her flailing hands. Legs like pistons pounded against hers and torpedoed them to the surface.

The shock of light and air revived her. Enough sense returned that she didn't try to struggle but allowed Lee to support her to the side and shove her up to safety.

Rolling over, Caitlin coughed painfully and sat up. A towel was pushed into her hands and she used it to mop her face. Finally she couldn't hide anymore and let the towel drop to her lap.

"Thank you," she croaked. Even to her the acknowledgment sounded grudging.

"Are you all right now? Do you need a doctor?"

"No. I'm fine."

He said, "That's why you're shaking like a leaf, I suppose."

"I'm not sh-shaking. It's just that it's a little cold in here."

"I see." And with that, Lee arranged the towel neatly around her shoulders and secured it there with his arm.

His skin, too, was chilled from the water and reminded her of the supple plastic flesh of a doll she had owned when she was ten years old. For an eerie moment, Caitlin felt a spurt of the intense love she'd lavished on that doll. Then the moment passed, leaving her more shaken than before.

"Did I say thank-you?" she asked.

"Yes. You were very polite."

He surprised a weak chuckle from her. It hurt her chest. "No, I wasn't, but you can say so. Have you forgiven me for being so mean to you at the dinner party?"

"Well, it depends," he said teasingly. "Are you going to be mean to me again?"

"N-no. No, I don't want to be mean to you anymore. Oh, Lee."

"What's this?" He tilted her chin.

The near-drowning had left her pupils so big they had swallowed the irises. Her face was milk white, except where her freckles stood out. Golden-brown spots even splashed across the web of blue veining on her eyelids and invaded the curve of her lips. He'd seen her pale before, but never like this.

She looked so woebegone. Unaccustomedly defenseless. He wanted to kiss the color back into her lips and make her strong again.

Caitlin didn't know what he saw in her face that caused his lips to part in a smile before they settled lightly over hers. It was almost a moth's kiss, passionless, she thought, on his side and over before it really began.

It waked in Caitlin the desire for another. She'd meant what she said. The last thing in the world she wanted to be was mean to Lee. Some part of her just couldn't accept that he was the enemy. Could she really blame him for doing his job? It wasn't as if there was anything about Jim for him to find out, and it was weeks since he'd kissed her properly. She wanted more than a taste.

Turning in his embrace until she was kneeling and facing him, she ran her palms firmly over his shoulders, sighed and pulled him possessively into a second kiss.

This one was liquid flame, his tongue coming confidently to fill her mouth, retreating and thrusting again, in an age-old rhythm. She went rapt, melting in his arms. Her hands remembered how to seek and give pleasure. They roamed over the wet mat of his chest hair and kneaded the hard slab of his back. But she couldn't recall ever experiencing this breathless heat or the wilful impulse to explore all of him until there wasn't anything else left to learn.

And all the while the kiss went on and on.

It was only when their lips reluctantly parted that it occurred to her how deeply the pitted concrete was denting her knees. With a bitten-off exclamation, she sat back on her heels.

"What is it? Caitlin, honey," said Lee in concern as he leaned forward. He put his lips on each set of reddening lines and dots. Somehow the act was every bit as intimate as the kiss they'd just exchanged. "Better?" he asked.

"Much," Caitlin murmured. "How's yours? The leg that got injured?"

"Doesn't bother me anymore, as long as I'm able to swim every day. Best therapy for it. That's why I'm not at the game," he said with a crooked smile. "I spent so much time standing this afternoon trying to impress you, the knee locked up on me."

She touched the crossword puzzle of scars. "You didn't have to do that. Was it horrible, having to leave the pros?"

"It was hard at first," he admitted, but his eyes were unclouded. "When you're a rookie, you think you're going to set the world on fire. It irks me sometimes that I lost the chance to prove what I could do. The poor guy who sacked me feels so bad I can't convince him to look me in the face anymore. That's the saddest part. We used to be friends. Anyway, I'd never seen the pros as a permanent career. I like the kind of work I'm doing now."

He brushed his cleft chin across her bare shoulder. The dark beard, which was starting to show, prickled deliciously.

"All right," he said decisively, "back in the pool."

"Back in the—oh, no. I've had enough for tonight, thank you."

"Come on, Caitlin. You know if you have an accident driving, you get right back behind the wheel before your nerves persuade you that you can't. Same with swimming. Back in the pool."

The water looked very deep. The artificial aqua color joined with the twinkling whitecaps to create a sudden brilliant, spinning chaos that made black dots dance in front of her eyes.

Dizziness put a catch in her voice. "I think I'd rather stay on the nice, comfortable concrete, if you don't mind."

He tucked a dripping curl behind her ear. His big hand cast a shadow across her eyes that relieved the disorientation caused by so much brightness.

Quietly he said, "I do mind. For you. Maybe I'd better explain something."

His hand continued smoothing her hair away from her cheek, her forehead. It felt remarkably good. She murmured, "Go ahead."

"I've found that there's a side effect to being a little stronger than most people. You learn to give the ones around you some space, or pretty soon you're all alone. Nobody likes being forced, even to do what's best for him. Or in this case, her," he said pointedly. "So although I think you're overreacting to falling in the water, and building it up into something worse than what it was, scaring yourself for nothing, the cure is simply to get wet again. But I'm not going to tell you to get into the water or else."

"Good."

"But Caitlin? I'm not really in the mood for an argument."

She looked at the angle of his jaw and got into the water.

It felt cool, then warm. She felt a surge of panic constrict her lungs. Lee slid in next to her. The five-foot mark brought the water up to her chin, if she stood on her toes. On Lee it barely crested the flat nipples hidden in his black patch of chest hair.

He eased behind her. "Okay, the object of this exercise is to remind you that water is your friend. Rest your head against my chest. Legs up, fine. Float. No, don't tighten up on me. Relax your back and tummy." His impersonal tone sounded just the right note from athlete to amateur, but his hands, gradually stroking the fear out of her muscles, belonged to a lover. They glided and soothed, and blood tingled to the surface of her skin wherever he touched, even though most of her back and all of her abdomen were modestly covered by her one-piece suit.

The water didn't seem like an alien element anymore, but instead dense and silky. Floating, Caitlin leaned her head back to say, "Lee? Thanks."

"What for?"

"This. I *was* scared. But now I'm not."

"I'm glad."

He didn't sound glad, though. His naturally deep voice had developed a rough, slurred edge. Twisting her neck so she could read his expression, she caught only a glimpse of the line of his jaw, the curve of a cheek, the downward slant of thick lashes beaded with tiny, sparkling drops of water.

"Is something wrong?"

Air whooshed out of him. "No, unfortunately, everything's great. Too great."

"That doesn't sound logical. I like it when things are great."

"Do you?" He flashed her a quick grin. The balance behind her head shifted, and Lee floated up underneath her. She could feel his upper body arch to gain all the support the water could give him. Masculine hair tickled her shoulder blades, and a firm, unexpected pressure startled her out of her pleasurable lethargy.

Long legs circled hers, paddling now and then to keep them both from sinking. The weight of his arms slung over her shoulders kept the seat of her bathing suit snug against that distractingly solid place where he was definitely aroused.

"What are you doing?" She felt a chuckle shake his chest. Hastily she amplified, "I know what, but—Lee, this position isn't possible!" He chuckled again. "Is it?" she asked uncertainly.

"Who said we were going to make love?" His hands slipped up her ribs. "We're just reminding you that you like to swim, remember?"

Lee's large palms completely covered her small, round breasts. He flexed them gently, almost idly. Water and fabric made a barely discernible film between his skin and hers. Her breasts grew alive, filling his hands, but everywhere else tension drained from her.

She drifted atop him, aware of his male body cradling her female one, very aware of the rigid bar of flesh that marked the reality of his attraction to her. The awareness was comfortable, for all the sensuality of water and skin and midnight. When was the last time she'd felt so pleasantly, mindlessly at ease in her own body? Ever?

Slowly she rolled in his embrace until they lay folded together like lovers. The kiss she gave him was only a grateful rub of the lips, but at the answering brush of his mouth a small whimper worked its way up from deep inside her.

"Time to stop," Lee muttered, and helped her scramble over the edge of the pool. "You choose the damnedest places to succumb to my charms, woman. Now what?"

"You mean—"

"I mean," he said patiently, "that I am not going to ravish you in full view of any professor who happens to want a midnight swim."

The image he evoked was irresistible to her sense of humor.

Caitlin made her voice full of disappointment. "You're not?"

"No, cat eyes, I'm not. I'm not going to ravish you at all—unless you ask me to. But you have to make a decision, Caitlin. When I make love to you—and that's what it'll be between us, you know that—*when* we make love, you'll have to want it as much as I do. And be willing to put it in writing. I think I'll want it notarized."

Caitlin let her middle finger trace the line of his brief black trunks. "Don't you think I want you?"

"Yes, I do. But something's holding you back. Intermittently, I grant you. Stop that," he added, imprisoning her fingers, "before I forget my good intentions."

"Maybe I want you to," Caitlin told him. Perhaps it was the shock of near drowning, but a sense of unreality had taken hold of her.

Where was her consciousness of Jim? Somehow since Lee had entered her life, she'd misplaced the burden of dead love she'd been hugging to herself for three years. Her body was unmistakably telling her that three years could be a very long time.

Inhibitions dissolved. She leaned forward so that her breasts, her erect nipples clearly outlined in the white spandex, grazed the little dark circles on his naked chest.

Lee's gaze dropped to the shadowy valley rising and falling with her quickened breath. He wondered if there were freckles even there.

"Maybe isn't good enough," he said with difficulty. How could he make her understand without scaring her back into her shell? She wasn't ready for real commitment yet; he could feel it. "No one-night stands. They aren't worth it. I don't want to spend myself like that, Caitlin. And I refuse to let you do it, either."

The water lapped and sucked beside them.

He said softly, "Do you know, I can count all—almost all your freckles? A drowned redheaded kitten with freckles. That's a hell of a thing."

Caitlin's frown quivered at the corners.

"I'll bet they called you Ginger when you were a kid."

"Not if they were smaller than I was!"

"And how many of them were?"

"Not very many," she admitted and smiled unwillingly. "I've always been a shrimp and hated it until now. But I love how tall you are next to me. It makes me feel . . . cherished."

"You are," he said and looked down at her quizzically. "I thought you were going to be mad at me."

"I was mad at you. Steaming. *Boiling*." Caitlin sat up straight. "You know, if I weren't sure you were on a wild-goose chase as far as Jim's concerned, I might be tempted to lose my temper with you. What's the idea of luring my stepson into that investigation of yours?"

Somehow Lee managed to rearrange his wicked good looks into the picture of angelic innocence. "I wanted to get to know Toby. He's a nice kid."

"He thinks you're next door to God. I got the rundown on your conversation in the gym. He made it sound like male-bonding heaven."

"I didn't bring up anything about the inquiry. Toby volunteered the information about those papers out at your cabin. I didn't even know about them until then."

"And I suppose he suggested our little trip to the lake."

"No, that was his friend, the blonde with the glasses. I'd say she keeps a pretty consistent eye on the main chance. She'll go far. But Toby seems capable of keeping up with her. Assuming they stay together, of course."

"They're only freshmen!" Caitlin protested.

Lee really did look like an angel, a seraph, one of the tall, gravely beautiful kind with sweeping wings. "Some people know who they want to spend their lives with after a day, or an hour, or a minute."

Caitlin could feel the flush start at the top of her bathing suit and inch upward. She searched her mind for a safer topic.

"Is it your fault I'm stuck on that crummy Oversight Committee?"

The reverberations of Lee's deep laugh thrummed through her whole body. "No, ma'am. I don't know why I'm on it, either. Are you sorry?"

She shrugged elaborately. "I'm becoming reconciled. It wasn't quite so easy to accept that you think of me as a *chaperon*...."

Lee's strong white teeth showed in an unrepentant grin. "To be honest, you're the one I was trying to lure. I thought a lake might be more conducive to—ah—"

"Fun and games? Gee, I don't know, hotshot, looked to me like you could have scored right here."

"Now, where did you learn to talk like that?"

"Library school." Caitlin jumped up, relishing briefly the sensation of being taller than Lee and the way his eyes narrowed to sapphire chips as he assessed the slim length of her legs.

She still wanted him—her body ached with yearning—but some remnant of common sense was nodding in satisfaction. They weren't taking a step that might be emotionally irrevocable. She felt suddenly, headily alive.

"I guess it's time to go home to my little boy and my cat."

Lee got to his feet. "You shouldn't be driving. You're still too shaky."

"Don't be silly. I'm fine." He didn't look convinced, so Caitlin stood on tiptoe and, with a mischief she couldn't control, licked the cleft in his chin. "Perfectly fine."

"You're a world-class tease!" he exploded. With a shriek of laughter, Caitlin made a dash for the ladies' shower, Lee close behind. Whether he would have chased her all the way she never found out, for just then the student guard appeared, mouth open and eyes goggling.

"Hey, you can't run in here! It's dangerous!"

As Caitlin skidded around the corner, she heard the student mutter, "Jeez, you'd think adults would know better."

She was still smiling when she approached the car, holdall swinging. A form detached itself from the trunk of a tree and, before she had time to be scared, stated flatly, "I said, you shouldn't be driving."

"Lee! Don't lurk. It's not the sort of accomplishment that guarantees popularity in a place like this. It so happens I'm a full-grown woman—"

"I'd noticed that."

"Stop changing the subject. I can drive myself home. So kiss me good-night and I'll see you tomorrow." She added, with a touch of anxiety, "Won't I?"

He pulled her close. It was too dark to see his expression, although some vagrant light gleamed off his eyelids and strong cheekbones, but she realized with a tingle that there was no possibility she could fail to recognize his touch, even without sight or sound to guide her.

"Yes, I will kiss you," he said, and he did. It was over too quickly. "If you won't let me drive you, I'll follow in my car to make sure you get home all right."

"You don't need to be this solicitous," Caitlin told him, rubbing her cheek against his sweater. "It's very flattering but not at all necessary."

"Humor me."

"A masterful man," she said with a sigh. "Okay."

And she enjoyed it when he held open her car door and checked the safety belt after she was seated. His hand lingered a moment where the shoulder strap crossed between her breasts.

She drove home very carefully, conscious all the time that the lights shining a steady ten feet behind her bumper were his. The red expanse of his sports car looked rakish next to her ultrarespectable Mercedes as it purred to a stop in the driveway.

Lee unfolded his length from the low-slung car and walked toward her, pantherish in his dark jeans. The scent of pine was sharp in the air. But it was the sight of him, black against the slightly less black night, that held Caitlin breathless. Without words, he drew her into a kiss so tender Caitlin's legs almost crumpled.

"That's so you don't forget where we left off next time I see you," Lee said.

"Not tomorrow?" Caitlin barely kept disappointment out of her voice.

"I got talked into putting in my two cents' worth at the team's postmortem session tomorrow morning. I should have said no, but it was nice to be asked."

"You really love football, don't you?" she asked quietly.

"I really do," he admitted. "And—don't slug me—but after some of the reading I've been doing over in the athletic department, I got the impression that you used to be pretty fond of the game yourself. Weren't you the statistician for the team your senior year?"

Caitlin bit her lip. "Found out."

"What happened? You *were* a genuine fan," he said positively. "I can't imagine you taking on that kind of job as a sorority girl trick."

"You mean to meet men? I asked for the position because I—oh, all right, because I loved football."

"You haven't answered my question," he reminded her gently.

"I'm trying," said Caitlin. "I sort of inherited an interest from my parents. My dad was Air Force and we lived all over, but no matter where we were stationed, he always followed his favorite teams. And my mom was worse. She ran the betting pool for the officers' club. It's amazing she never got Dad cashiered from the service."

"They sound great."

"They were. The commercial flight they were on crashed when I was twenty. After that, I guess I watched football as a way of feeling closer to them. Then when Jim died, too, it was easier to blame football than myself."

"How could you possibly consider yourself responsible for any of those deaths?"

Even in the darkness, his gaze was too penetrating. Caitlin looked away. "I know I was being stupid. The thing is, my parents were on their way to visit me here at school when their plane went down. And Jim—"

She stopped, then started again. "If I'd been a better wife, less passive, more—more whatever it was he wanted, he might not have concentrated so hard on work. Not relaxing killed him. He was always challenging some sort of unstated goal."

Even in bed, she thought sadly. The sense of closeness, of fulfillment, of the richness of emotion that enveloped her when she was with Lee had been completely absent from her marriage. Jim had been too busy striving to meet his own standards of excellence to share himself with her except in the starkest physical way.

Lee's arms went around her fiercely, comfortingly. "Type A's tend to be like that. Work is their mistress, and wives or husbands just cope the best they can," he said. After a while, he added, "Now, me, I'm a type B. Or even a C."

"There's no such thing as a type C," said Caitlin, her words muffled in his shoulder.

Lee planted a kiss in her hair. Her tense, too-still form was starting to warm to life again. If her sense of humor was asserting itself, she was coming back to him, away from the past.

He wondered if his opponent for Caitlin's love wasn't a ghost, after all, but the guilt she seemed to have carried away from her husband's funeral. On the whole, he preferred to fight the guilt. At least it existed in the present, even if its roots were buried in Caitlin's stubbornly active memory. A ghost, on the other hand, especially one regarded by his wife as a paragon, was a hard adversary to beat.

"No type C? Are you sure?"

"Positive. I could look it up for you if you like."

"No, that's okay. It just means that I'm unique."

Caitlin laughed shakily. "I'm willing to admit that."

"I was joking."

"I wasn't. Want me to recite your stats?"

"Shh. You'll turn my head. I do want to succeed at my assignment, though. It'll mean a promotion to the Seattle office."

"Is that important? I mean, is it important to you?"

Lee exhaled. "It would involve a lot less travel, less legwork. I'd get a chance to make policy, instead of merely implementing it. And I'd be able to have a home, not just a home base. Those things are important to me, yes."

He hoped she'd say something, anything, to show how the idea of a permanent, stable home—with him— affected her, but instead she snuggled closer and remained silent.

After a while, she said, "What else are you doing tomorrow?"

Like her, he kept his tone matter-of-fact. "Appointments all afternoon and a boosters' dinner till the wee hours. I'd gladly skip out early on that except my boss wants the conference to be visible so I got roped into giving speech number one."

"What's that?"

He chuckled. "Its title is 'The Morality of Football,' bolstered by anecdotes from my pro days. Speech number two is 'The Immorality of Football,' also illustrated by anecdotes from my pro days. Speech number three is still in draft form, but it'll be 'The Education in Physical Education.' You heard the beginnings of that in committee."

Caitlin fingered the part-rough, part-soft nap of the wool of Lee's sweater. "It was impressive. And it sounded *true*. You're a wonderful speaker."

"Did you think so? Your hair was standing on end. I kept expecting to be turned into stone by your Medusa glare."

"Liar!" accused Caitlin. "You know all you have to do is look at me with those baby blues and I go all soft and gooey like maple sugar candy."

"I like maple sugar candy. And in case that was cynicism talking a second ago, the things I said yesterday were true. At least I believe them."

She lifted her face to his. "I wasn't being cynical. I don't think I could be, about you."

"Cait!" His lips were so close she could feel their heat on hers. "If I kiss you again I won't be able to stop. So I'm going to let you go—" very slowly he released her "—and watch you walk through that door."

"Would you stop acting as if I were a feebleminded thirteen-year-old?" Caitlin asked in exasperation.

"Am I being too Neanderthal and protective? I suppose it's because there's something not quite real about all this."

That's how I feel, too, Caitlin thought. The combination of soft damp autumn night and Lee was magical.

Lee continued, "Maybe it seems too good not to evaporate in the light of day. Chances are I'm making a big mistake giving you time for second thoughts."

8

LEE CONTINUED to be busy "chasing whispers," as he called it, and Caitlin saw him only on the run. They managed to steal a few tormenting kisses in the library stacks, where Caitlin tempted fate several times, testing how far she could take her newfound sensuality before Lee called a halt. It was irresistible to try to seduce him after he'd declared so firmly they wouldn't make love, yet. Once, though, when she could tell he was as aroused as she was, he groaned in her ear, "You're lucky this is a public place," and spanked her lightly as they emerged from the semiprivacy of the philosophy section.

On the job, students in the first barreling enthusiasm of the semester kept Caitlin's feet and fingers flying with their questions, demands and youthful untidiness. At home, Toby's preoccupation with something-or-other precluded much discussion. If he noticed the subdued glow that shone back at Caitlin from her mirror, he didn't comment on it.

She refused to let Lee's absence dampen her small, steady flame of happiness. Without really thinking about it, she began to spend more time in the kitchen than the living room.

As the long weekend approached, she sang as she unearthed suitcases from seldom used closets and grinned mischievously as she packed several of the la-

cier underthings Auretta had talked her into buying.
They weren't the most appropriate garments she owned
for a weekend whose ostensible purpose was scrub-
bing and hanging storm windows at the cabin, but it
was just possible, she thought, that she and Lee could
put them to good use. Brenda and Toby weren't going
to be around all the time. The two of them would take
walks and go boating and sleep over at Brenda's. And
while the teenagers were pursuing activities that would
provide themselves with privacy, they'd incidentally
create some for Caitlin and Lee.

Which meant there wouldn't be anyone to chaperon
the chaperon.

Auretta gave Caitlin a too perceptive glance from
under her frizzy yellow bangs as they sipped tea during
the afternoon break on Thursday. "You're looking
pert," she said.

"Thank you."

"Over in personnel, they had to scrape the director
off the floor when he heard you were taking a day off.
All set for this exotic weekend?"

"Just about. Are you sure—"

"Yes, dear, I'm sure it's no trouble to take your cat for
you. No, I'm not planning anything particularly wild
and woolly myself. As behooves an old bat lady librarian, I shall settle in with my ISBN numbers and
catalog cards and devote my precious free time to the
greater glory of dear old Tall Pines. Wondering all the
time just what you're doing."

"Me?" Caitlin practiced looking unintelligent. "I'm
only the chaperon."

Auretta surveyed the casual twist of Caitlin's hair,
which allowed an aureole of coppery tendrils to cluster

around her face, and the green knit dress clinging discreetly to her excellent figure. "A more ridiculous description I've never heard in my life. I was right about that dress, wasn't I?"

"You were right about all of them," Caitlin said frankly. "And thank you again. You give me hope. Don't you have anything on for the weekend? What about your professor friend?"

"He may drop by," Auretta said airily. "We'll see. He's awfully slow on the uptake. You had him pegged on that."

Caitlin smiled dreamily. "Sometimes slow is better."

Auretta raised her brows. "Caitlin, child, you are a hopeless, cliché-ridden romantic. I never thought I'd see the day."

"To be honest, neither did I."

"Now, if I wasn't forgetting!" Auretta leaned her elbows on the table. "Did you find that professional magazine I left on your desk? I circled an ad for you."

"Yes, I saw it," said Caitlin with a small smile.

"For heaven's sake, don't you start getting discreet. It's so irritating."

"Sorry." Caitlin turned the cup with her little finger. "The ad was very interesting."

"Caitlin! Are you or are you not going to apply for the job at the football conference archives? It has everything—better pay, executive responsibility, it's in Seattle—"

"My house happens to be in Spokane."

"Your *man* is going to be moving to Seattle," Auretta pointed out.

"I don't know that he is my—and how do you find out these things, anyway? You know more about my love life than I do!"

"Oh, I ran into Lee Michaels one day." Auretta's smug smile told Caitlin that the accidental meeting had probably been deliberately engineered. "We had an extremely productive talk."

"I can imagine. Do I have a single secret left to my name?"

"You shouldn't be so suspicious. Although if I were fifteen—oh, all right, twenty—years younger . . ."

Reproachfully Caitlin said, "Control yourself. Remember you already have a gentleman friend."

"I do remember. Unfortunately. What about the ad?"

No matter how far afield Auretta's Southern exuberances of speech might take her, she never lost sight of an unanswered question. Caitlin laughed and said, "I sent in my résumé on Monday."

At five o'clock, Caitlin loitered at the reference desk a trifle longer than necessary after briefing her substitute. It was just possible Lee would find a minute or two to spend with her before his next appointment.

A boy with a pink bouffant coiffure wanting to know what year "the *Hindenburger* sank" had her cornered when the close-cropped black curls moved into her field of vision. The sight of Lee distracted her enough from her professional calm that she said sharply, "I beg your pardon?"

"The *Hindenburger*. You know." Caitlin's amazed stare drove his voice up an anxious octave. "It, um, it sank, right?"

Lee's suppressed chuckle did nothing to restore Caitlin's poise. Cheeks scarlet, she whipped out an almanac and flipped through the pages till she came to the citation.

"The dirigible *Hindenburg* exploded during docking in 1937," she read coldly.

"Oh," said the student. "Then it sank." He went off, happy.

The boy was barely out of earshot before Lee's bass laughter boomed through the high-ceilinged space. Caitlin collapsed into her chair, head shaking and face in her hands.

Lee finally choked to a stop. "Do you get many like that?"

Caitlin considered. "Yes."

"Heaven help us. How'd that specimen get admitted to college, anyway?"

Caitlin looked innocent. "I thought he was a football player."

Lee flashed her a blue-eyed glance. "I don't think so. I'd remember the hair."

They strolled out of the building, together but not touching. Caitlin, her five senses stretching, was aware of every movement Lee made, the length of his stride, the shift of muscle under his tight-fitting sweater and jeans. They emerged into the golden moment that sometimes climaxed late afternoon in the Northwest. It suffused the landscape with a warm glow even as the long shadows of twilight heralded the beginning of night.

Lee watched her hair take fire from the shimmering light. "How'd you know I'd fall helplessly in love with the color of your hair?" he asked softly.

"Just one of the—" she searched for a pompous enough word "—the inestimable benefits of being born Irish. I didn't plan it that way."

"I'm disappointed."

The simple phrase, spoken in his black velvet voice, was full of meaning. Caitlin looked up to see if he was teasing or only half-teasing, and found him studying her so intently her heart turned over. He definitely didn't look like a man who would wait much longer for a woman to make up her mind. In fact, he gave the appearance of someone whose plans for the weekend would dovetail nicely with hers.

Caitlin's brain kept spewing up lightly ironic sentences to disguise the reaction welling from deep within her. The tenderness that clothed his virility left her defenses scurrying to protect her from hurt, but they weren't working. *No one-night stands*, he'd said. A weekend affair was precisely what she kept telling herself she wanted, what she needed.

But Caitlin no longer believed that herself.

Some lingering remnant of the armor that had shielded her for so long caused her to shrug and say, "So it goes."

They'd come to the parking lot. Lee asked, "Where's your car?"

"It was so pretty, I walked today," she answered. "See, I can cut through here and take the alleys home. That way I can find out what my neighbors are hiding in their backyards."

"You really like it here, don't you? In Spokane, I mean."

Caitlin thought of the application she'd mailed to Seattle. It was too soon to talk about it.

A faint smile eased Lee's somber expression. "Home is where the heart is."

"Yes, naturally," Caitlin agreed, and gave him a warm squeeze of the arm to make up for being secretive.

"Naturally," he repeated and pulled her roughly to him.

He didn't kiss her, but after a few moments, one of his long fingers delicately pushed a lock of her bright hair back from her cheek. The last trace of—not ill-humor, but some sort of thorny humor—vanished from his mouth.

"When should I pick you up tomorrow morning?" he asked.

"Brenda's parents are early-rising freaks, from what I understand. Toby wants to ride with them, so it's just you and me."

"That sounds cozy," he said. "What time?"

"Around seven, I'm afraid."

"I'll try to survive it. Is there someplace reasonably secure to park the car?"

She explained the parking arrangements at the marina and added, "We've never had any trouble. But are you sure you want to risk your sleek beast?"

"Is that what you call it? Fair enough. Yes, it sounds safe. Cars are made to enjoy, not coddle." His fingertip touched her bottom lip. "See you tomorrow."

She saw him sooner than that.

Toby walked into the house after nine o'clock to find Caitlin sitting on the cat carrier, brooding.

"That French guy would love you," he said.

"What French guy?"

"You know, the sculptor. You look just like that statue, except for the pedestal."

Caitlin looked down at herself and realized she'd fallen into the classic pose of *The Thinker*. She grimaced and stood up.

"Rodin notwithstanding," she said, "Flame caught sight of the carrier and took off out of here like I'd offered her a nice complimentary dose of bubonic plague. She's supposed to go to Auretta's tonight, but I don't know what to do. I can't go anywhere overnight with her missing."

"Calm down, Ma. Did you try calling?"

"I have called. I have searched. I have put a whole dish of chicken livers on the back stairs. That cat is not buying it."

"Okay," said Toby in a soothing voice. "When do you need to have her at Auretta's?"

"Now."

"Right. I'll go walk around and see if I can spot her. After all, she doesn't associate me with the cat cage, just mean old Ma. You phone Auretta to say there's been a slight hitch in your plans. Good thing it's not too late, Lee Michaels gave me a ride home in his car. We've got plenty of time, so relax."

"Relax, he says," Caitlin muttered as she dialed. She spared a fleeting smile for Lee, transporting her lamb home in his fabulous car. Briefly she wondered what they'd talked about, but then Auretta's high-pitched staccato, made nasal by the connection, came on the line.

The older woman assured her she'd be ready and waiting for Flame whenever the cat arrived. Toby stopped to say he'd checked one side of the street and was about to embark on a tour of the other.

Caitlin scooted him on his way and went upstairs to double-check her packing. A peek into Toby's room revealed his suitcase open and as empty as it was two days ago when she put it there. She was tempted to begin his packing, too, but decided that any right-thinking college freshman would not thank his stepmother for that kind of assistance. Then there wasn't anything to do but go back downstairs and pretend she wasn't there so maybe Flame would come home.

It wasn't too hard to sit quietly when she had Lee to think about. He really was amazing. Not just gorgeous, not just intelligent, but nice. He wasn't an empire builder. And that was nice, too.

The doorbell put a halt to her musing. A quick view of the clock told her it was almost ten.

"Hi." Lee's grin was forced. "Did you by any chance lose your familiar?"

"Flame! How did you know?"

"It would be kind of hard for me to ignore, to tell you the truth. Your nice little kitty is in my car. She will not come out of my car. Believe me, I've tried everything short of a nuclear blast as an inducement." His tone was joking, but Caitlin gasped as he stepped into the hall light.

"Your hand! And, Lee, there's blood on your sweater! Did Flame do that?"

"I'm afraid so. It's probably my own fault. She'd already made it clear she didn't want to come out from under the seat. So I thought I'd use a little physical persuasion. Next time I'll know better."

Caitlin took his uninjured hand and led him upstairs to the bathroom near her room. "The first-aid stuff is all in here," she said. Setting soap, antiseptic ointment and adhesive bandages in a row, she watched as he washed the scratches on his hand and wrist.

"Are they very deep?"

"Nothing fatal. Most of them won't even need a bandage."

"What about your chest?" She couldn't keep the worried note out of her question. The sight of blood didn't normally bother Caitlin, but seeing Lee's blood shook her.

He finished applying first aid to his hand and pulled his sweater off in one easy motion. Caitlin grabbed a washcloth and swabbed at the double row of welts that arced through the triangle of fleece that grew on his chest. The marks just missed the brown dots on either side. Her skin was white in comparison.

"You're so tan," she said.

He grinned. "The name was originally Micheletti. Italian clear through. My great-grandfather anglicized it when he came to this country."

"The scratches are red but not bleeding," she said uncertainly. "I don't think we need to do anything else to them."

"So that's all I get for risking life and limb to retrieve a witch's familiar? Not even a kiss to make it better?" Lee asked, reaching around her for his sweater.

The action put his nipple right in front of her nose. Caitlin brushed her lips over the tantalizing spot. She didn't intend the fleeting caress to lead to arousal but it did, and instant liquid heat trickled through her. As her body nuzzled closer to his, craving more contact, she felt his own unmistakable response.

A door crashed. "Ma!"

They drew a deep, common breath. For an instant, their eyes met, sapphire against gold, blurred with frustrated desire.

Caitlin rested her head against Lee for a last strengthening moment before she called out, "Up here, Toby."

Adolescent feet galloped up the stairs. "Where—oh, hi, Mr. Michaels. What happened to you? Ma, did you do that?"

Toby's teasing grin was unclouded by any darker emotion that Caitlin could detect.

Lee replied, "As a matter of fact, it was another female in your family who did the damage. That cat of yours."

Toby's grin widened. "Flame? You found her? Great! Ma loves her cat. She'd have called off the trip if Flame didn't show up."

"To be precise, Flame found me," said Lee, his baritone deepened even further by the folds of his sweater. His ruffled curls emerged and he added, "Perhaps you could coax her out from under the seat of my car. Here." He fished keys out of his jeans pocket and tossed them to Toby.

Toby lit up. "Sure!" he said ecstatically and dashed back down the stairs. The front screen door whapped behind him.

"You have just made his century," Caitlin told Lee. "He will probably kiss the upholstery."

"Good. Then I can kiss his stepmother." He did so, thoroughly. "You know, it's ridiculous, you being anybody's stepmother. How have you coped?"

They followed Toby's steps more sedately.

"One day at a time, left foot, right foot... Toby needed me right at the time I was most adrift. After Jim died, I couldn't eat ice cream or go to a movie because it seemed like a betrayal of the grief I owed him. When I told myself Jim would have been appalled at the way I was behaving, it was worse, because I was using him as an excuse. Survivor's guilt. This is the first time I've even taken a vacation day."

For the space of a heartbeat, Lee wanted to turn back the clock, save Caitlin the pain he could hear echoed in her soft, low voice. If a wish could have done it, he would have given her back Jim. Then he felt a surge of triumph. She was *talking* to him. Finally she was allowing him a glimpse of the intensely private Caitlin no one else got to see.

Very gently he said, "It wouldn't help to turn into a professional widow."

Caitlin wrinkled her forehead. "I know. It took a while, but eventually I decided all that grief was an extravagance I couldn't afford. Toby was as lost as I was, and he didn't have anybody but me. These past few years I think he's raised me as much as I've raised him. Of course, he won't be needing me much longer. Certainly not after the next few years."

"Years?"

The incredulous note in Lee's exclamation escaped Caitlin because Toby eased into the hall just then with a seething apricot-and-white bundle tucked securely under one arm.

"Lead on, Ma."

Once Flame was incarcerated, spitting and writhing, in her carrying case, Toby looked back and forth between Caitlin and Lee. "How did you know Flame belonged to us, Mr. Michaels?"

Lee felt rather than saw Caitlin's back tense. Neutrally he said, "I dropped in one night to discuss some things with Caitlin. About the case."

"Oh, yeah? Well, I guess I'd better get the ferocious feline over to Auretta's. See you tomorrow, Mr. Michaels."

"Toby." Caitlin held out her own keys. "Here, take the Merc."

"Okay!"

He left at a little less than his usual breakneck speed out of consideration for Flame, who was glaring through the mesh-covered hole of her carrier. Caitlin turned to Lee, smiling.

"So why do you want to keep us a mystery?" he demanded.

Her bright look faded. "What—"

"Why don't you want Toby to know we're—interested in each other, for want of a better phrase?"

Her hand lifted, then dropped. "I haven't been 'interested' in a man before. Since Jim, I mean. Toby has feelings. I want to spare them."

His mouth tightened. "I was hoping we'd gotten past this point. Toby's dad has been dead for a long time. Do you think he isn't aware opposite sexes attract? He's eighteen. The kid's got plenty of hormones and the imagination to know you've got them, too."

Caitlin felt the blood drain from her face. "What's that supposed to mean?"

"Now what—Cait, that is *not* what I'm getting at, and you should know it. Toby adores you, but not that way. It would be obvious—even if I hadn't already met Brenda."

She relaxed. "All right, then."

"Aren't you confident of Toby's emotional maturity?" he continued mercilessly.

"Toby's very mature!"

"So he is," Lee agreed. "A big boy. And you're a grown-up girl. You can't stay dependent on him forever. Honey, I hate like hell saying these things to you. Can't you see—"

The concern was so plain on Lee's face that Caitlin's resentment vanished. "Yes," she said unhappily. "I'm trying, anyway. But believe it or not, it was Toby's choice to live here at home and go to Tall Pines. We could have swung it if he'd wanted to live on campus, even another campus, where he'd have to pay tuition. Of course the time will come when he goes off on his own. Just not quite yet. Please, Lee, can't you understand?"

Her hand went out again, and this time he took it. His fingers sent a sustaining warmth through her.

"I wish I could figure you out," he said.

Caitlin opened her hazel eyes wide. "I'm not that complicated."

"Hah. For Mother Machree, you're a lot of woman."

She straightened her shoulders. "I know. That is, I know I've been . . . coming on to you more than a nice girl would."

"Have I ever indicated I thought you were less than a nice girl?" Lee asked.

"Only once or twice. Stop laughing and listen to me. I have a confession to make." Caitlin paused to put her thoughts in order. "You've probably noticed I find you attractive."

"That would be consistent with the way you've been behaving," he said solemnly.

"Ever since that night at the pool I've been taking advantage of you."

"Well, you've tried."

"And that's what I'm trying to explain. I haven't been afraid to show you how much I want you because you promised we wouldn't become lovers. So it's been safe for me to tease and touch . . ." She gulped at his expression. "I'm being honest."

The naked hunger in his face eased a little. "I know. It means a lot to me."

"I can't let this weekend start in a—a dishonorable way. Whatever happens between us."

Lee ran his fingers through his hair. "You've lost me again."

"I'm falling in love with you."

The words fell ringingly between them. Time seemed to stand still, shift its focus and start fresh in a whole new prism of experience. Caitlin drew an audible breath and went on. "And I wanted to tell you that if you would like to make love with me, I'd like it, too. Not pretending or teasing or manipulating or any of those destructive things. Just . . . loving."

Her straightforwardness affected him in the most direct way possible. He wanted to pick her up and find a level surface—any level surface—and drown in her desire.

Jim's house was the wrong place and with who-knew-how-many minutes before Toby came back it was no less the wrong time, but...her eyes looked so bright and vulnerable; the honesty her admission had taken had obviously cost her something. He knew he had to give her something in return.

Letting his fingers play in her soft curls, he said, "I want to touch you." His kiss was leisurely with a sensual deliberation that coaxed her tongue into a slow exploration of his mouth. He pulled back to whisper, "Tell me where you want me to touch you."

"Lee, I love it wherever you—"

"You're not listening." He made his voice low and tender. "The only kind of pleasure I want right now is pleasing you. We'll let me be selfish another time. Tell me."

The old sweatshirt Caitlin had thrown on for the evening's chores had faded in patches. They varied from gray to an unbecoming noncolor. The baggy hem dipped in several places. Definitely not seduction material. Lee didn't seem to notice. His tapering fingers massaged their way over her scalp, down the nape of her neck to her shoulders. The sweatshirt suddenly became a totally unnecessary, bothersome encumbrance.

In a murmur barely loud enough to be heard, she told him what he wanted to know. Her sweatshirt didn't block the warm path his hands took to the clasp of her bra. Apparently the bra didn't pose much of a barrier to a determined man, either, because he pushed it out of the way and then Caitlin found it too difficult to concentrate on anything except the intimacy of Lee's hands on her breasts.

He'd never caressed her before without the civilizing restraint of at least one garment between them. She couldn't think, couldn't breathe, when he used the pads of his thumbs to circle the soft little tips until they stood out in wanton peaks. The touching would have been nothing, a meaningless physical indulgence, without the sense of closeness she always felt with Lee. This wasn't just hands and breasts and labored panting in a moment of stolen privacy. It was Lee cherishing Caitlin.

As it was, when he spread his palms around the yielding flesh and caught her swollen nipples between thumbs and index fingers, a strong current of desire surged downward, flooding her lower body with a consuming ache that extended to her legs.

Lee felt her tremble and knew he had to call a halt. His own control could only stand so much. He reclasped her bra. The words dragging out of him, he said, "See you tomorrow."

"Lee Michaels!"

The outrage she put into his name drew a look of singular beauty from the planes and angles of his face.

"Yes, Cait, I'm in love with you, too. You can't doubt how I feel about you." He cupped her hand in his and brought it close to feel his fullness straining to meet her touch. "But the fact is, that postadolescent of yours is going to come bouncing in here any minute. Let's face it, you'll be miserable if he catches us doing any of the things we really want to do. So I'm going to leave. Now. Before I recover my sanity and decide I don't want to trade you for another cold shower."

9

To her amazement, Caitlin woke Friday morning to realize that she'd slept deeply and dreamlessly. She'd crawled into bed about twelve with the expectation of lying sleepless all night. But the next moment, Toby was pounding on her door and a mist-muted sun was pouring pearly light through the window.

"Ma! Ma!"

"Okay, okay." Caitlin yawned as she swung her legs to the floor. "I'm getting up."

"It's six-thirty. We've got half an hour!" Toby yelled.

"Yikes!" Caitlin cast a horrified glance at her bedside clock, grabbed her robe and made a dash for the bathroom.

Her hair was a trifle more riotous than usual as she and Toby, laughing, ran for the two cars that idled in the driveway. Lee was getting directions from Brenda's parents. Everyone exchanged greetings. Toby piled into the back seat next to Brenda, leaving Caitlin smiling up at Lee.

"The body is very sexy," she drawled, trailing a finger in a sensuous design on the bumper of his car as the others drove off, "but has it got any storage space?"

He grinned in comprehension. "Honey, this body's got everything. Where's the gear?"

He refused to let Caitlin carry any of the boxes or suitcases out of the house, so she contented herself with murmuring several times, "This stuff is never going to fit." But somehow, with Lee doing the arranging, it all did.

They started a bare quarter hour after the first car, with a sack of groceries that couldn't be shoved in anywhere else under Caitlin's feet. Lee drove with the kind of quiet confidence that didn't rely on speed to impress. Caitlin relaxed. It was lovely, she thought, to lean back and divide her attention between Lee's profile, absorbed in the unfamiliar road, and the hilly terrain as they climbed toward the state line.

"Pretty country," Lee observed after a long silence.

Clouds hung low, hiding the tops of mountains. Away from towns and farms, long-needled, downward-spreading pines took over the landscape. Occasional leafy trees and shrubs were brushed with autumn reds and oranges, like splashes of accenting color in a painting dominated by somber green.

"Do you really like it?" Caitlin asked. "A lot of people think the evergreens are depressing, but I love them. They're so mournful and dignified, as if they know they're left over from a past age. In the spring, when the snow melts, you can find thousands of scraggly seedlings poking up out of the forest floor."

The road unwound before them, rising straight and slate-gray over a summit.

Caitlin said, "I guess they remind me that no matter what the odds, life goes on."

Once over the peak, the highway descended sharply into the bowl of a valley. At the bottom lay the lake. Its pewter surface was abruptly brightened to blue by the sun, which had burned a widening hole through the fog.

"Give me my dark glasses, will you?" Lee requested. "They're in the glove compartment. The sun on that white mist really produces a glare."

Caitlin picked through a welter of maps and tissues until her fingers closed on the unmistakable shape of a glasses case. At the same time, they dislodged a prosaic little package that slid into Caitlin's lap.

"Oho," she said. "What are these?"

Lee glanced over. "I imagine you know what they are. I stopped at an all-night drugstore before turning in yesterday. They aren't something I carry around with me on the off-chance," he told her.

Caitlin gently replaced the box and handed Lee his sunglasses. He slowed the car to enter a village clinging to the edge of the lake, then made the turn to the marina, where Caitlin directed him to the moorage where Brenda's family kept a gleaming cabin cruiser.

"Admire the boat," Caitlin said in his ear before she slipped out of the car.

Lee said complimentary things and asked intelligent questions as the men loaded the provisions and the women sat in deeply cushioned deck chairs. Caitlin would have pitched in with the work, but Barb, Brenda's plump and heavily made-up mother, seemed to regard the division of labor as normal.

Once they got under way, Caitlin enjoyed the smooth speed and gusty wind so much that she didn't notice their course until the engine cut back and the big boat glided toward a strange pier with a taut sky-blue awning.

"Not much like ours, huh, Ma?" Toby asked.

Barb was wearing the steely smile of a determined hostess. "We couldn't let you go without brunch!"

"I'll—I'll just tell Lee," said Caitlin.

She went forward and drew him a little away from Brenda's father. "We've been shanghaied for brunch," she whispered. "Don't blame me, I just found out."

"Let's not stay too late," he replied. "How are you doing?"

"She's incredibly boring."

"They're a well-matched couple. Poor Toby. How's he stand it?"

Caitlin tried not to laugh. "I guess you were right. He must be in love."

Brenda's father, Roy, proudly showed off his possessions in the split-level cottage, which was better equipped than the Stewarts' home in Spokane. The kitchen contained a dishwasher and garbage disposal. The bathroom had been copied from an interior decorating magazine. The living-dining area boasted a glass wall.

After a while Caitlin was able to see a vagrant wisp of cloud pass over the sun, and exclaimed, "Oh dear, the weather's worsening. I hate to cut this short, but I'm a terrible coward about boating when the water's choppy."

Everyone made suitable noises of regret. As Brenda backed the boat away from the dock, Caitlin said, "I hope your parents don't mind being stranded until tomorrow."

"Oh, no. Daddy'll be on the phone all day and all night, telling his friends about Lee. And Mother'll take off her girdle and watch the soaps. We've got a satellite dish."

Neither activity sounded like anything worth leaving Spokane to do, but Caitlin was aware that not everybody was susceptible to the rustic charms of her own summer cabin. She frowned at Lee. "I never told you about our place—"

"Here it is," Toby interrupted.

Brown shingles almost blended into the background of untamed wilderness. Almost, but not quite. There was no hiding the fact that the structure loomed three stories high and was just as wide. Or that it was as ramshackle as it was large. All the outer windows were innocent of glass. Screens gaped and paint was peeling. Moss grew out of once-impressive cedar roofing.

"It's better inside," Caitlin promised.

"This is your cabin?" asked Lee appreciatively. "You could house a battalion in there."

"Twelve bedrooms," Toby said with relish.

Caitlin added, "And one Spartan bath. It's not very gracious living, Brenda."

Now that she'd seen from Brenda's family cottage how she was used to roughing it, Caitlin was fretting about the girl's reaction, but Brenda gave Toby a glowing look as the craft eased up to the weathered dock. "I think it's neat."

Everybody pitched in and it took little time to stow the groceries in the kitchen and the overnight bags at the top of the stairs.

"Anybody interested in lunch?" Caitlin asked.

"I'm awfully full," Brenda said.

"Why don't we just plan on an early dinner?" Lee suggested.

Toby's face fell. Caitlin said unkindly, "Don't tell me, you're hungry. Stuff yourself on potato chips."

He sent her his hundred-watt grin. "Okay. Want to explore, Brenda? We can start in the kitchen." Off they went.

Caitlin looked up at Lee defensively. "The accommodations are a little rugged."

"I don't think so. There's a fireplace, a refrigerator, a stove and a nice selection of beds."

"The stuff you want is in there," she said, pointing him toward a small room built onto one side of the house. "Enjoy."

The filing cabinet shared space with an ancient tasseled lamp, a manual typewriter so old, Lee saw with fascination, that the letters didn't occur in standard order and a collection of molting stuffed owls. A layer of sand lay over everything. Outside, the sleepy slush-slush of water approaching the shore provided a pleasant distraction.

An even stronger distraction was the sound of Caitlin moving around the house. Half-overheard joking comments exchanged with Toby and Brenda alternated with bumps and thuds. Reminding himself that the sooner he finished his distasteful task, the sooner he could go find out what Caitlin was up to, Lee opened the top drawer of the cabinet.

After two hours of squinting at faded penciled notations about long-since-graduated players, Lee yawned and closed the lowest drawer in relief. Nothing. He couldn't help but be glad. Not even for Caitlin would he compromise a case, but he'd flinched from the thought of finding something in her own vacation home that might tarnish Jim's memory.

Anyway, what did he have? The current coach was a nonentity, the kind forgotten as soon as the last yearbook was signed. An unimaginative type, the poor guy had inherited a bad situation, not masterminded it. No, the corruption had begun during Coach Stewart's tenure. The issue was how much Jim had known and how Lee was going to prove it.

He wished like hell he had a solid piece of evidence one way or the other. As things were, the only damning documents he'd seen so far were copies of several clearly incriminating letters. He wasn't a handwriting expert, but the scribbled notes he'd just inspected certainly bore enough of a resemblance to the letters to justify asking for an expert opinion. Even so, none of it was exactly hanging proof. Nor was the crime a capital offense. Just the same old, sad story of promising athletes introduced to soul-destroying greed at far too young an age.

A big, fat question mark might be the most satisfactory end to the investigation as far as Lee's relationship with Caitlin was concerned. But the idea of turning in an inconclusive report irked him. There'd been too many similar scandals lately. His bosses were out for blood. And Lee wanted that promotion. When he thought about coming home to Caitlin every night he wanted it a lot. The whole mess was complicated by the fact he'd never doubted—in fact, he was positive—that Caitlin shared with him an itch to know the truth. Anything less than a definite vindication would send one pint-size redhead through the roof. Dusting grit from his hands, he remembered the traditional fate of bearers of bad news.

The thumps had gradually been getting closer, and Lee realized they were now directly overhead. Leaning out through a slit in the screen to get his bearings, he caught sight of something descending and dodged just in time to avoid a cedar chip as it hurtled to the sandy terrace.

Someone was, literally, on the roof.

Rounding the house, he was treated to the vision of Caitlin, the bottom of her jeans furred with stray bits of moss and bark, balancing on the unsteady slates while she looped the corner of a tarp over a hook.

The canvas secure, she turned, saw him and smiled.

"I know you're going to think I'm being Neanderthal again," he said, trying not to speak sharply, "but couldn't you have subcontracted out this particular job? It doesn't appear too safe up there."

"The roofing does seem a little spongier this year," she admitted blithely. "Shingles keep coming loose."

"I know," he said with feeling. "Where's Toby?"

"One floor up on the other side, doing the same thing I am. He wouldn't let Brenda or me up there with him, so stop looking so censorious. We've got to get the windows covered before snow flies." Caitlin shivered. "It feels like it might any minute."

"If it's all the same to you, I'd rather not see you fly. Would you come down from there? Please?"

Her heart-shaped face mischievous, she walked crabwise down to the eaves. "I hope you intend to catch me," she said and slid feetfirst into his arms. They tightened around her.

"Now that I've got you on terra-sort-of-firma," said Lee, "maybe we could think of a nice, leisurely activity to while away the afternoon." His hand crept up to stroke the back of her neck. "Something that would relax these tension knots, work the kinks out, limber your muscles. . . ."

The hand knew just how to massage her into jelly, but she tried to resist. "Not with Toby and Brenda so close—oh! Do that again. It feels so good. . . ." Her eyelids drooped.

Lee continued to knead that exact same spot.

"As a matter of fact, I was going to ask them to join us."

Caitlin's eyes snapped open.

"We can't play football with just the two of us," he said reasonably.

10

CAITLIN GROANED as she measured her position. Only a few yards separated her from the badminton net, which was serving as goalposts. Unfortunately Lee seemed to be occupying all those yards. She'd never appreciated before how big he was, how solid and how many arms he had.

They weren't playing by any particular rules. Lee and Toby had appointed themselves defense, on the grounds that there wouldn't be anything left of the two petite women if the men took the offense. Naturally Caitlin and Brenda responded by launching various kamikaze plays in an attempt to score, but this was the closest either of them had gotten so far.

"Time-out!" Caitlin called. "I want to confer with my teammate."

She ostentatiously hugged the ball to her chest as she huddled with Brenda. She'd already caught Lee and Toby nudging it backward when they thought no one was looking.

"What do you think?" Caitlin whispered.

"I think we're dog meat," answered Brenda. "Unless—I saw a movie where this girl lifted her shirt and froze her blocker and her team won the game."

"Are you kidding? I'm the one who would freeze. It can't be more than forty degrees out here. Besides—" she jerked her head toward a large, flat-bottomed boat slowly approaching "—the tour boats always pass right by our beach."

"Then we're doomed," Brenda said.

"Probably," Caitlin admitted. "But I want to wipe the smirk off those two gorillas' faces just once. Keep Toby occupied—and keep your shirt on."

They resumed their positions. Caitlin counted off a completely imaginary set of signals, and dived straight past Lee's legs. At least she tried to. At the last moment, Lee stepped sideways into her path to stop her headlong sprawl toward the goal line. Her shoulder caught his bad knee and Lee crumpled.

Caitlin screamed even before he hit the ground in a soft spray of sand. Abandoning the ball, she crawled frantically to his side, crying, "Lee, did I hurt you? Your knee—"

He reached out an arm, pulled her on top of him and grinned into her startled face. "Gotcha." Turning his head lazily, he squinted at the ball. "I'd say you're a couple of feet short."

Caitlin wrenched herself free. Too angry to speak, she took two precise steps toward the ball and kicked it in a high, narrow arc over the net.

A burst of applause rang out over the water. The tourists aboard the boat clapped and waved.

With her head held high she glared at Lee. "You guys can continue to entertain the peasants all you want. I'm going to fix dinner."

The kitchen was at the front of the house. As she started the propane grill and unwrapped chicken, she heard Lee say, "You shape up pretty well, Toby. Can you throw a football to the person you're aiming at?"

His voice unusually level and serious, Toby answered, "When I want to."

Caitlin wielded her spatula to the steady slap and grunt of pass practice. Toby's high school years had passed with no sign of interest in competitive sports. She was suddenly unsure whether that was because he felt none or because he sensed how much resentment Caitlin had developed against the game that had obsessed his father.

The other three finally came in when she called them for the meal. Everyone was ravenous after the outdoor exercise, and laughed and made toasts with what Toby named "vintage root beer" from a case left over from last summer.

After dinner, the wind fell slightly and Brenda and Toby zipped up their parkas and went to sit on the end of the dock in the concealing darkness.

"Better them than us," said Lee, tossing another pine log on the fire.

"This is lovely," Caitlin agreed, tucking her legs under her on the shabby sofa. "You look nice in your sweaters. All three of them."

Sitting very close to her, Lee laid an arm across her shoulders. "Thanks. The only drawback I can see to this house is that it does tend to get a little nippy."

"Just a little," she said. Leaning back, she rubbed her neck against his forearm. Even through the layers of wool, she could feel his muscles tighten in response. "There's not much point in trying to make it habitable in the winter. No access by road. It's strictly for summer. I suppose I ought to sell it."

"Why? Do you want to?"

"No, I have the terrible taste to love it. But it's so impractical. Have you ever seen such an old barn? The screens are falling apart, the roof's coming down piecemeal. We'll probably have mice nibbling our toes tonight."

Lee smiled at her. "Those are all things that are easily fixed."

"That's what you think. I found a mouse in the oven while I was cleaning."

"Which one of you screamed louder?"

"He didn't get a chance," said Caitlin. "He's more like a mouse mummy. Dead for months."

"Does your use of the present tense indicate that the mummy is still haunting the stove?"

"What I like about you, Michaels, is that you're perceptive."

She felt him chuckle. "I suppose I'll have to be heroic and dispose of it before we get any breakfast in the morning?"

"*Very* perceptive."

"If I get rid of the mouse and the screens and roof are replaced, will you hang on to the property?" he asked.

Shyly, she said, "Do you want to?"

"Well, it's secure right down to the water, with nothing to break that's not broken already. Another pound or two of sand tramped inside isn't going to make any difference. One adult could supervise the whole beachfront from the porch. In other words, perfect for kids."

She moved her head. A gleaming sheaf of red-gold strands reflected the light from the fire in a thousand dancing highlights. He drew a breath. "Just in case either of us—or both of us—wanted to think about kids."

The thought of having Lee's children sent a warm shiver through Caitlin. She watched the pulsing, ruddy glow illuminate his features, the strong nose and chin, the mobile mouth.

He said, "Do you know, with your eyes all big and serious like that, you look just like that cat of yours. Where did you get eyes that color? Nobody has golden eyes."

Caitlin smiled. "They're only hazel. It's not a very romantic color. Not like yours. I've never seen anyone else with eyes so blue. They're really beautiful. All of you is beautiful."

Lee's mouth quirked. "It's always bothered me to get a compliment on how I look, as if that was all people would ever notice about me. Or worse, as if they could somehow make me over into the person they imagined I ought to be to match my looks. Once when I was in grade school, a few other boys and I did some damn fool thing—stole duck eggs from the city park—and every single one of those kids caught hell for it except me. They let me go because they couldn't believe such a nice-looking kid could be a juvenile delinquent. After that I was an outcast in my class. Not one friend."

Caitlin didn't like the bitter lines that deepened Lee's cheeks. With a flash of intuition, she realized he was seeing that normal little boy, confused and resentful of an adult world that treated him as if he were extraordinary and cost him his companions in the process.

"That's when I started concentrating on sports," he added. "The coaches didn't care if I was pretty or not."

"Are you wondering if I'd be here with you if you were . . . less spectacular?"

Caitlin could feel the tension gathering in him, vibrating through his arm, down his side and along the length of his thigh.

"I suppose I am," he said and sighed. "Not because I have doubts about you, honey, but because I've gotten used to being judged on superficialities."

Caitlin nodded. She remembered the way he'd reacted at the Mallorys' ghastly party. This was important to him.

She said slowly, "Of course I've noticed how handsome you are. How could I help it? When I'm near you, or think about you late at night, I—I burn up wanting to touch you. Whether I'd have been as immediately attracted to you if you weren't quite as gorgeous as you are, I have no way of knowing. What I do know," she said, taking his face between her hands, "is that I love the person who lives behind your eyes. And once I'd gotten to know *him*, I'd have wanted to be close to him and make love with him, no matter what he looked like."

She stretched to give him a resounding kiss on the forehead. "So there!"

Lee rested his cheek against her hair. She was always doing something unexpectedly right.

He'd never admitted this particular vulnerability to a woman before. He never could have except to her. The curse of good looks was a concept that generally produced smirks, if not downright laughter, and he supposed it was better than being damned with ugliness. But he'd been the pariah, or found himself used as a sort of trophy too many times.

Yet all Caitlin had had to do was acknowledge the pain and banish it to some faraway place where it didn't matter. "Cait, Cait, I love you, too."

They sat quietly for a while. Lee wondered how he'd lived before Caitlin brought him this sense of peace.

Finally he stirred, shifting his arms slightly, and the dying fire allowed a draft to blow against Caitlin's flushed face.

"At least I can offer you an electric blanket for the night, Lee."

He kissed her temples, her eyelids, the sensitive places just under her ears. "I can think of cozier ways to stay warm."

She turned her head so his next kiss fell on her eager lips. Not quite twenty-four hours had gone by since she'd felt his mouth move against her mouth, his tongue gently, sweetly, test the edges of her desire and then, when her lips parted, seek her tongue. Not even a whole day, but it felt like forever. He tasted so good, like barbecue sauce, wood smoke and root beer.

The day's growth of beard shaded his face. She traced his jawline, prickle by prickle, with a slow, exploratory finger. "I suppose it would be futile to say I couldn't be seduced by you."

His hands were sliding inside her pullover and the turtleneck beneath. "You may not realize it, but this is definitely a mutual seduction. You do powerful things to me, lady."

"You make me feel . . . Lee, I've never felt this way before." She pulled away. "It scares me a little."

"It ought to," he said. "This is real life, Caitlin. Forever time. Promises and a ring time. Those are the things I want with you, and if you can't commit to them—to me—then we're wasting something very special. All or nothing, Caitie Cat Eyes."

"Are we talking a long engagement?" she asked hesitantly.

"No."

At the uncompromising reply, she moistened her lips. "I know this is going to sound really dumb, but I need to think about it for a while. I—I don't seem to think very well when you're touching me."

His stern look vanished and was replaced by the familiar teasing glint. "Don't tell me 'this is so sudden.'"

"Well, it is! We haven't even known each other four weeks." In a very low voice, she added, "It's not that I haven't dreamed of making love with you. In color. Because I have, but—"

"It's all right, love. In fact, until you're ready to make a commitment, I have absolutely no intention of sleeping with you."

Caitlin choked. "That's sexual blackmail!"

"True."

"Lord, you're unscrupulous."

"I'll use any foul means to entice you into marrying me," he said, leering and twirling an imaginary mustache. But behind his playacting, there was a hint of basic, primitive hunger that told her he might not be as hard to seduce as he claimed to be.

Locking her hands behind his neck, she raised her eyes to his and startled herself with a huge, uninhibited yawn.

"Bedtime for you," said Lee decisively, and stood, lifting her up with him and continuing to hold her in his arms.

"Lee! Your leg! The kids could come in any second."

"Stop wriggling," he ordered. "I keep telling you, my knee is fine. Even if it weren't, your little weight wouldn't bother it." He swung her gently, as if to prove it, and Caitlin tightened her grip.

The physical temperature, she thought confusedly, might be less than ten degrees above freezing, but the sexual temperature in the room needed lowering fast. She wanted nothing so much as to cling to his overwhelming strength, to court his rising need until she was soft and liquid and hot and slick and could abandon herself to learning love from his hard, lean body. His arms felt like oak, and supported her as easily as if she were a baby.

Babies. A dark-haired baby with Lee's smile and his deep blue eyes. The picture drew on instincts she'd never allowed loose rein before today, and combined with her desire it produced a small, frustrated noise.

Be sensible, she told herself. She and Lee had just come to the conclusion it would be wise to wait.

Caitlin was very tired of being sensible.

She forced a slightly taunting note into her voice. "You just like showing off your muscles."

He gathered her closer. "I do like showing off for you. Go ahead, laugh."

"It doesn't make me want to laugh. It makes me all trembly inside." This was not going to cool things off appreciably, she thought. "If Brenda and Toby walk in right now, their eyes'll bug out."

"I doubt they'd be that shocked. What do you think they're doing out there?"

"You're wrong," Caitlin said demurely. "Brenda told me that under the circumstances it would be extremely uncool."

Lee deposited Caitlin outside her bedroom with a kiss so tender she actually felt dizzy and had to catch the doorframe as his broad shoulders and neatly clipped head disappeared down the stairs.

Slouching with his feet crossed on the scarred coffee table, Lee stared into the fire and listened to the explosive pop and sizzle as it sent little orange tongues licking at pockets of resin in the half-dry wood.

Upstairs was the woman he wanted, while he was sitting down here with hands thrust into his pockets, trying to will away the swell of longing her scent, fading in the smoky air, kept bringing back. He knew he could retrace his steps, knock on her flimsy plank door and talk his way, past her reservations and his own convictions, into her bed. Electric blanket be damned. The heat they could generate together was what they were both slowly dying for.

The only thing that stopped him was the cold certainty that Caitlin's independence was too valuable, too much a part of herself, to diminish. He could tempt her into a night of love, but not the lifetime of loving he wanted with her. She had to come to her own decision in her own time.

Nevertheless, as the logs crumbled to embers and the waves hushed along the shore, Lee wondered if he was being the prize jackass of the universe.

A NEW RESORT HOTEL had been built across the lake. Caitlin hadn't seen it up close yet, but from her window its twinkling lights transformed it into a fairy tower, insubstantial as mist. Real as dreams. Perversely, her drowsiness departed the moment Lee left. She changed into her new nightgown. The silk fit like another, sensual skin from breasts to thigh. Its spaghetti straps hadn't been designed for fall weather, and shivering, she pulled the electric blanket from the bed and swept it around her shoulders. The cord trailed after her as she sat with her chin propped on her folded arms, supported by the windowsill.

Toby and Brenda came inside at last. The acoustics of the house made it impossible for her not to hear as they used the bathroom, then went to their separate bedrooms. She grinned in the darkness. Trust Toby to be considerate, and Brenda to be discreet.

Her old-fashioned alarm clock, ticking noisily in the darkness, didn't have an illuminated dial, but it seemed very late before she heard Lee's heavier tread creak on the stairs. The small, homely sounds he made preparing for bed were familiar yet unfamiliar, pleasant but just unaccustomed enough to raise a prickly awareness that there was a man in the house.

Her man, if she wanted him.

She tried to consider Lee objectively.

If he wasn't perfect, he came awfully darned close. The problem had never been him, but her. Long ago she'd decided she was a failure at the kind of intimacy he could create just by breathing next to her.

Caitlin's thoughts turned to the first time she'd ever slept at the cabin. The electric blanket had been set at high then, too. Though the vacation had been planned as a family outing, Jim had been busy.

Perhaps, she thought, the time had come to face the fact that her wholesale avoidance of men since her widowhood hadn't been an act of homage to the wonderfulness of her marriage. Staring at the fairy lights across the water, she silently admitted that she'd blamed herself for its shortcomings and trusted herself too little to try again.

Neither birth certificates nor marriage certificates come with guarantees, dummy, she told herself. You did the best you could and prayed that things turned out and took the blessings God gave you. Lee might not be perfect—there was, after all, his annoying habit of usually being in the right—but he was perfect for her. And she would just have to try to be perfect for him.

So the problem wasn't a problem at all.

Her decision made, she tucked the blanket tidily over the bed, and let herself cautiously into the corridor, listening. The habit of mother-henning was too strong to break. Toby's snoring would have identified his whereabouts even if she hadn't already known which room was his. Brenda, who gave such an excellent impression of being hard-boiled, had brought with her a dented night-light in the shape of a pink bunny. The crack in Brenda's tough facade made Caitlin glad for Toby's sake. If there was a vein of human tenderness in his self-possessed blonde, he'd figure out how to mine it.

People needed tenderness. They needed a sense of belonging with someone, of knowing they were valued. She needed Lee. Now.

Lee's door was shut. Inching it open, she heard nothing, not even shallow breathing. She'd been sure this was where he'd dumped his bag, but . . .

"I assume you're not a burglar," he said out of the silence.

She slipped all the way inside and leaned on the door to close it. A fingernail-size moon shining through the unglazed window supplied the dimmest light possible.

There was only enough of a glow to distinguish large objects—like the bed, and Lee. He sat up, his bare skin gleaming in the faint light.

"I was cold," she murmured plaintively. "I hoped you might warm me up."

"Caitlin," he said, sounding strict, "do you know why I said it wasn't any use for you to try to seduce me?"

She crossed the drafty floor, stopping at the side of the camp bed and clamping her arms to her sides to conserve the little warmth left in her limbs. "N-no," she told him, her teeth beginning to chatter.

Lee looked at her. In spite of the uncertain illumination, she was giving a convincing performance of a woman freezing to death. Common charity required that he rescue his love from the elements. That clicking noise must be her teeth. He couldn't make out what she was wearing, but it would have to be Arctic underwear to withstand the cross-breezes in this place. However, it didn't take a soothsayer to figure out what was going to happen once they were both warm and unclad under the same covers.

And that was fine by him. She was tired of waiting, and so was he. In fact, he was rapidly forgetting why waiting had seemed like a good idea in the first place. He was no more than human.

"On second thought," he said at last, "if I told you we didn't belong in the same bed, I must have been crazy. Come here."

Pushing back the blanket, he grasped her chilly hand and pulled her down next to him. She came all in one piece, as if she were literally frozen. Instantly, she curled into the heat of his body, and he exclaimed remorsefully, "Hon, you're practically an icicle. Why didn't you tell me?"

"I d-did tell you," she reminded him.

"You should have told me louder. I thought you were at least half-kidding. Here, get your feet between mine." Not only did he imprison her feet between his own, but he tucked her hands into the warm crevice between his thighs. Knowing what an icy shock they must be, she tried to pull her hands away, but he scolded, "Don't be foolish. It's okay. That's the warmest place I've got."

She discovered smooth skin slightly roughened by hair and hard muscle, and felt herself grow loose and flexible as his body heat seeped into her.

"Maybe the windows would be better with glass in them," she mumbled into his shoulder.

"No, that would wreck the ambience. Besides, how would I get a sexy-eyed witch to fly into my arms in the dead of night if not through the window?"

"I don't suppose she'd just walk down the hall? If she happened to know where you were sleeping and needed rather desperately to, um, practice her arts on her lover?"

"Oh, no. Too ordinary. My witch is a pretty complicated lady."

He wrapped both arms around her and rubbed all the parts of her body exposed by the nightie. The friction felt wonderful. She sighed when he paused long enough to arrange the blanket around her ears. There was a smile in his voice, and a deeper, more urgent note than usual as he said, "Nothing about my witch is simple. But I want to make this simple for her." His hand moved. "And this. And this. Simple and easy and just exactly right."

"You always know what to do to make me feel good." She cuddled closer, although the cold was no longer a concern. Lee's palm swept big, lazy circles over her back, up and down, and farther down. His other palm found and encompassed a breast, tightening for a moment as if he were staking a claim. Then his fingers very lightly investigated the shape of her nipple through the sheer barrier of the nightgown.

The slippery stuff bunched and crinkled under his searching fingertips, adding the tease of silk to the profounder excitement of skin against skin. Lee liked the gown, he liked it very much, but he liked the thought of Caitlin out of it more.

He shifted to let her hands, now definitely warmed, go free. They rose in a single caressing motion to where his body showed how thoroughly aroused he was.

"Sweetheart." The endearment emerged as a groan. "If you do that, we'll be finished before we actually begin."

"Really?" She sounded immensely pleased. Her touch grew busier. "I'm glad you sleep without any clothes on. Skin is nice."

He found the hem of her gown and began to tug it gently over her slender hips. "My thought precisely. Sit up for a second." As he extricated Caitlin from the cobwebby material, he realized for the first time how very little the garment had covered. To distract himself from her activities, he said, "Not that I'm complaining, mind you, but why on earth didn't you put on something like long johns before you came flying through the night? There's nothing to this thing." He tossed it to the end of the bed.

"Vanity," she said simply. "I was hoping to try it out on you. It was all I packed. I wanted you to think I was sexy."

"Well, if that's all you're worried about . . ." He settled into the pillow, pulling her with him. "I knew you were about the most sensuous little bundle I'd ever seen the minute I laid eyes on you."

Caitlin let her gaze drift over his chest. Under the pale moon, his black hair made an interesting geometric shadow. She ran her hands over it. The individual hairs curled tightly enough to tangle into a close-packed mat, but the whole was unbelievably soft.

"That's the most deeply male chauvinist remark I have ever heard."

"Do you mind?" His mouth was pliant, his beard bristly where they brushed her face.

Both made her sigh happily. "Not if you mean it."

"You know I mean it."

He smoothed kisses over her lips, her throat, her breasts, as if he had to entice her by slow, gentle degrees to what she already wanted with fierce hunger. It seemed to her that all the moments they'd spent together, every teasing word or passionate touch, had been sufficient foreplay. Lee's readiness couldn't have been more obvious, while a feverish rush of damp sensation to the apex of her body sent uncontrollable tremors racing through her that must have been apparent.

But he just kept on lavishing those unbearably sweet, undemanding caresses over her impatient body. His gentleness made her feel as fragile as the porcelain sliver of moon shedding its light through the window, when she wanted to give him the strength of the passion that had been building in her ever since they'd met.

More wiry than the luxuriance on his chest, the hair on his legs chafed the delicate skin of her inner thighs in a way that said man-woman very clearly. The message went directly from flesh to flesh. Lee's fingers suddenly flexed in the twin softness of her buttocks, and she curved her leg around him to feel the fascinating, rough texture of his calf again.

Caitlin's frankly sexual movement opened her to his touch. His palm soothed, the tips of his fingers probed. She arched, throwing her head backward in a wanton, revealing gesture as new to her as the cascading pleasure that followed the motion of his hand. Lee woke responses in her she'd never known she had and she imagined where they would lead as she burned and ached to hold him closer.

Lee wanted to hold back, to spin out this first, precious time with Caitlin, to bring her to impossible delight in herself, in him, in what they were capable of together. She hadn't spoken a word of love since she'd blown into his room like magic on an updraft of the shiveringly fresh, clear air. But there were other ways to speak of love than with words.

He wooed her with his lips, taught her cherishing with his hands, told her about the value he placed on her with the depth of his gentleness. The long preparation had him almost shuddering with anticipation, and her increasingly wild, sweet reactions to what he was doing only intensified the demands of his own body.

"Witch." His voice was a slurred rumble. "Can you feel what you do to me?"

He lowered himself onto her so she could become used to the solid length of his arousal as he fumbled for the package he'd placed in the drawer of the nightstand.

The seconds it took him seemed like an aeon to Caitlin. She heard her own ragged breathing, not much louder in her ears than the hammer-blows of her heart, and felt a sharp ache of emptiness inside her. Lee had created the empty space and only he could fill it. The words *I love you* and *I never want to live without you* trembled on her tongue, but she bit her lip to keep them unspoken. If Lee wanted to play at fantasy, then she'd play, too.

All she could see of the lover who'd haunted her dreams for weeks was a silhouette, and that also helped the pretense. She became an enchantress, flying to the mate she'd chosen on narrow moonbeams, indulging in earthly love with the broad-shouldered mortal who'd tempted her from her solitary ways.

But with the first warmth of intrusion, the fantasy paled next to the reality. Lee was real. Her body cradled his as if that was what they had both been made for. Nothing in the world mattered except the way she fit over him, he fit into her.

The joy of finally feeling Lee where she wanted him to be changed swiftly into vast, aching pleasure. She started moving deliciously, irresistibly, in response to his careful thrust. The hard muscles of his back rolled under her restless fingers. She could sense the power he was restraining and the effort it took for him to keep himself in check.

A spring coiled inside her, wound tight by the exciting weight of him atop her. Containing all the power that was Lee pushed the spring past the point Caitlin could bear. Her body rebelled; the coil sprang free; waves of pure sensation spiraled through her.

Lee felt her convulse beneath him, heard the choked gasp that marked the crest of her passion.

It was too soon. He'd meant to take her much more slowly. In fact, he'd intended to be a model of patient, loving endurance and outlast his own most grandiose fantasies, because he knew how long it had been since Caitlin had visited a man's bed. She'd told him there had been no men since the end of her marriage, and his Caitlin never lied. She wasn't shy. That had been made compellingly clear on a number of occasions. Still, he hadn't known what her response would be to anything but the gentlest lovemaking.

The quick way she took fire astonished and then delighted him. If he could force himself to maintain a leisurely, moderate pace, he thought he might even bring her to completion again. But nothing about the feel of Caitlin under him, around him, encouraged moderation.

And he was so tired of waiting.

She subsided into softly pulsing quiescence. Tiny, contented noises came from her throat as she slid a long, openmouthed kiss over his collarbone. She was as open and natural in her satisfaction as she'd been in passion. Lee groaned, "Caitlin," to warn of what he was about to do, went rigid and drove as deeply into her welcoming flesh as he could go. She surrounded him, absorbed him, accepted him for exactly what he was, and all the roaring need and desire and love that was in him poured out in a burning flood of pleasure.

After a long time, he said, "Waiting was a really stupid idea."

"Yes," she agreed drowsily.

"You're sexy as hell, did you know that? I couldn't hold back any longer."

She nuzzled his neck. "I didn't want you to."

Lee disentangled himself from her only to release her from his weight. Then he carefully arranged his large body around hers, spoon fashion, and rested his chin on her hair.

"Still, that wasn't all I hoped to . . . I'll make it up to you, sweetheart, I promise."

His self-deprecating tone prodded her love-drenched mind, and she blinked. The strengthening predawn light met her gaze. Stirring, she rolled over to smile at him.

"You have absolutely nothing to make up. You didn't take advantage of me, you know. I sneaked into your room, remember?"

The coming of a new day reminded her that it was time to move, before Toby and Brenda began to roam the house. She kissed Lee softly, preparing to get up.

He responded with a light, admonitory pat on her bare hip. It was distinctly friendly, and also proprietorial to a degree that filled her with a warm sense of belonging. She kissed him again, rubbing her lips back and forth over his just because it felt so good.

"Caitie—Caitie, you're going to have to stop that. You need some sleep. There are circles under your eyes." He kissed the circles, then her heavy eyelids, then, despite the fact her mouth parted expectantly, her nose. "I'll wear you out later, sexpot. You'll just have to take it on faith. I know I hardly set any endurance records for you. A standard for speed, maybe."

That jarred her. "Lee, believe me, I've never gone looking for someone to set records with. Never. You're a wonderful lover. *The* most wonderful lover." She reached out to reassure him with her hands, but he caught and held them over her head.

"I have to admit I generally have delusions of—not grandeur, but at least proficiency," he conceded. "And I'll prove it to you after you've had some rest. Now face the other way, honey, or I'll forget I intend to be a gentleman. Again."

Obediently, Caitlin turned, feeling the brush of his stiffening flesh in the small of her back. She wanted very much to stay, and not to sleep, but she had to go. More important, she had to explain to Lee.

"How blunt do I have to get?" she asked in mock despair. "Nothing that felt like that has ever happened to me before. I thought I knew—but I didn't. You said you could make everything simple and easy and *right*. And you did. I love you so. If I wasn't able to show you that . . ."

The shaft pressing into her back grew fuller, but the rest of Lee relaxed suddenly, as if she'd finally said what he wanted to hear. His muscular arms remained loose but persistent around her waist. He dropped a chaste kiss on the top of her head. "Oh, you showed, all right. I had to turn down the electric blanket."

The return of his teasing relaxed her tension, and with it the last remnants of any ambition to leave his bed.

Feebly she protested, "I really ought to get up before the kids—"

"Sleep now."

"But—"

"Sleep."

Lee's deep voice, softened to a growl, was impossible to resist, and Caitlin slept.

11

THE STEADY CHUG-A-CHUG of a passing lake barge filtered through the other morning sounds—birdsong, a businesslike hum from a few hardy wasps, the ever-present wash of waves along the beach. Cold licked at Caitlin's cheeks, but the remainder of her was lapped by a sense of warm, indolent well-being. Her eyes didn't want to open.

She started to burrow deeper into the pillow when a weight on her shoulder stopped her. Lee's whiskery face pressed intimately into her breasts. His heavy body lay lodged against hers; they must both have shifted during their few hours of sleep.

Easing away by cautious inches so she wouldn't wake him, she heard shouts and the thud of running shoes on the dock outside. Toby and Brenda. With a fervent hope that neither of the teenagers had peeked in on her unoccupied room, Caitlin slid to the floor and reached for her nightgown. Lee seemed deep in sleep. He sprawled at the very edge of the bed. Her stomach tightened with a gurgle of laughter as she realized she must have chased him across the bed while they slept.

The soft click of the door closing signaled Lee that it was safe to open his eyes. Caitlin had been so quiet stealing away that he'd decided to let her think she hadn't wakened him at her first stir.

It was a little early for a confrontation, anyway.

Lee rolled over, encountering a patch where Caitlin's scent lingered on the pillowcase. Brow creased in thought, he began his usual wake-up stretches, limbering his mind at the same time he loosened his muscles.

He did not regret last night. He would have needed to be a sadist or a masochist to have sent Caitlin away unloved. A grin lightened the concentration on his face as he coaxed the kinks out of his bad knee. In this case, the gentlemanly act of sharing bodily warmth had been its own reward.

But he couldn't deny he'd lost a prime bargaining chip in convincing Caitlin she couldn't live without him. Or gained one, depending on the point of view. Contemplating her uninhibited sensuality had an inevitable result on his body's condition. Sighing, he grabbed his pants. He'd wondered if spending a night with Caitlin would defuse his lightning-fast responses to her.

Apparently not.

CAITLIN CRACKED OPEN the oven door and then quickly banged it shut again.

So Lee wasn't perfect, after all. He'd forgotten to throw out the mouse.

Smiling to herself, she tore a paper towel from the roll and opened the oven once more. Gingerly, she gathered up the remains.

"I hope that's something for breakfast. I'm starving," said Lee behind her.

"You'd have to be, to eat this," she replied.

He took a closer look at what she was holding. "Oh, for—honey, I'm sorry. To tell you the truth, I had other things on my mind last night."

"I should hope so," she said decorously.

"Here, let me," he urged, plucking the towel from her hand. "Where do you want it?"

"You can throw it out back, I guess, as a warning to the other mice."

"Am I going to get breakfast anyway?" he asked.

"Blueberry pancakes," Caitlin said, indicating a bowl of purplish batter. "Somehow, I can't work up a lot of enthusiasm for using the stove. Maybe I'll put the skillet on the barbecue instead." Lee started out the back door, and she added without raising her voice, "Do you think you'll want a civil or a church ceremony?"

There was a pause of perhaps three heartbeats, then Lee said, "What?"

Caitlin dipped a spoon in the batter to test its consistency. "I said—"

"I heard what you said. Look at me."

Balancing the spoon carefully so it wouldn't sink, she turned to Lee.

"Do you mean it?" he demanded, suddenly harsh.

At his expression, fierce and searching, Caitlin felt her knees begin to knock. Forever time. This man wasn't accepting anything less. Slowly, shyly, she nodded.

Still Lee didn't move, and the breath squeezed out of Caitlin in a rush. Behind the beauty which time would only deepen, not erase, she read insecurity. He hadn't been unsure of himself the day they'd met. He'd been charmingly aggressive and a little bit cocky. His doubts were as lovable as his confidence, but today of all days he should feel safe in the virility that never failed to stir her femininity. She wanted to give him back his magnificence.

"Generally speaking," she said lightly, "couples usually kiss or something right about now. Only if you feel like it, of course. I wouldn't want to start nagging you so soon after the engagement. But if you were to feel like it . . ."

Lee let Caitlin's soothing nonsense flow over him. He'd come down intensely curious about her state of mind, ready to insist that they reach an agreement over the status of their relationship, but mouse removal and blueberry pancakes hadn't struck him as a very promising prelude to discussing marriage. Caitlin had surprised him again.

This was real life, no doubt about it.

Laughter danced in his blue eyes as he held out his arms.

She shrieked and backed away. "Lee, for heaven's sake, look out with that thing! Don't touch me!"

Lee stared blankly at the mouse as he became aware that Toby and Brenda were crammed together in the doorway. Caitlin dissolved into giggles.

"Here, get rid of this," Lee said to Toby. Crossing the kitchen in two strides, he wrapped Caitlin in his arms.

Forgetting that they had witnesses, she pressed as much of herself as she could against his comforting length. The feel of him was something she needed, like food or air or water.

"Love," she whispered, identifying the natural element that had been lacking from her life for so long. She took his face between her hands. "Oh, Lee, I need to love you."

"I know," he answered softly. "Like some overwhelming force it's far too late to resist. I think it was too late for me the moment I first saw you."

"Jeepers," said Brenda soulfully.

"Yeah," Toby agreed.

Reminded of their presence, Caitlin gave Lee an extra hug before she pulled away. "I, uh, I guess I'd better get breakfast on," she said with an uncertain smile at Toby.

"We'll do that," Brenda offered.

"You two go sit or take a walk or whatever," Toby added. "We can handle stuff in here. Congratulations!"

Blushing furiously, Caitlin muttered, "Lee and I are engaged."

Toby snorted. "We'd just about figured that out, right, Bren? Go on or we'll never get to eat!"

"Don't use the stove!" Caitlin shouted as Lee dragged her outside.

They were both warmly dressed, since the cabin was as windswept as the white-tipped lake itself. Strips of thin, pastel cloud, scudding over the hills that crowded in on the water, were rapidly paling, but the hills themselves remained silhouettes, misted black, untouched by the rising sun.

Caitlin watched Lee's breath make frost as they strolled to the edge of the beach and leaned against the pump house.

"What do you want to do today?" Lee asked, tickling her ear.

Caitlin whispered, "You know what I want."

He twisted his fingers through her hair. "Much as I like Toby and his girlfriend, I wouldn't mind ditching them for a while myself."

Caitlin gave him a wide grin. "Don't you remember? They're spending the next two days with Brenda's parents."

"Yes, but we need transport," he said, frowning at the boat as it bobbed on the unquiet water. "Sometime today I intend to toast you in champagne, not root beer."

"There's a hotel in the village that's supposed to be nice," she mentioned. "We could ask Brenda to drop us there in time for lunch. I—we can always come back here before winter sets in to finish closing the place up."

"Come and get it!" called Brenda from the nearest window.

The return trip to the village was accomplished at record speed, since Brenda shot Lee and Caitlin one swift look and opened up the throttle. Toby hesitated a moment while hoisting bags onto the wharf, to say to Caitlin, "I'm glad for you, Ma. I mean it. You deserve to be happy."

He turned before she could answer and became very busy with a canister of gasoline.

Lee declined an offer to help load his car. "You two go ahead and enjoy yourselves," he said firmly.

"Say thank-you to Barb and Roy for us," added Caitlin.

Without Toby's things, stowing the luggage took very few minutes. Lee glanced at Caitlin and said, "Okay, where's this hotel?"

It was located at the water's edge and expensively decorated in Northwest chic with high beamed ceilings and a big fireplace of native granite. The subdued gold coloring on walls and floor bespoke a combination of good taste and money.

That money was spent here she couldn't doubt. One of the couples treading the modern parquet floor would have been recognized anywhere in the Western world, and everyone was wearing the kind of carefully casual clothes that made Caitlin grateful Auretta had browbeaten her into shopping not so long ago.

"Hungry?" Lee asked.

"Yes."

"We can find out if they're serving lunch yet—"

"It's not lunch I'm hungry for."

Lee lifted her fingers to his lips for a surreptitious kiss. "My, how you talk, madam librarian. Are you sure?"

"More than sure."

While he dealt with the receptionist, Caitlin tried to control the sensual glow she was sure everyone in the lobby could detect in her. She was concentrating on a picture of what Flame's silent stalk and needle-sharp claws could accomplish in Auretta's apartment when Lee touched her arm lightly, leaving a small, lingering sensation of heat.

"This way. What are you thinking about? You look like you just swallowed a canary."

"That's an unappealing snack idea. Actually, I was thinking about Flame just now. I was imagining her strung up on Auretta's loom like a spider in a web."

"Let's hope not."

"Oh, I don't know. Might serve Auretta right. She can be kind of pushy, you know. She pushed me to see more of you."

"Fine woman," said Lee. "Salt of the earth." Caitlin giggled, and he added, "You can always call and find out how they're getting along."

"I suppose I could, but I'd feel sort of silly calling long distance to check up on my cat."

"Why?" Lee smiled down at her. "Don't you love your cat?"

Caitlin sighed. "Yes. Yes, I do."

"Then call. But not," he said, throwing open a door, "right now."

The room was spacious, decorated in soothing variations of green. It was warm and inviting, but all Caitlin could focus on was the bed. Its more-than-king size dominated the space. Her throat went dry.

The lock clicked firmly into place under Lee's hand.

"Now," he said, with a rasp that deepened his voice till she could feel it vibrate through her chest, "we are finally, completely alone. Just you and me. No one knows we're here. Not cat-sitters, not stepsons. My God, you do look like a cat. Your eyes are glowing. A rare, desirable, cat-eyed witch who's put her spell on me."

Caitlin shook her head so the curls swayed slightly. "I'll be whatever you want. But I'd better warn you—when you touch me, you're the magician, and I'm the one under *your* spell."

His voice dropped even further. "Then let me see all of you. Last night was . . . there aren't words. I want to look at you, find out everything about you. . . ."

Her eyes locked on his. Backing up so he could look his fill, Caitlin let her fingers drift from one button to another, loosening, uncoupling, discarding. The cardigan went first, then the underlying blouse, then the slacks. When the final wisp of nylon floated to the carpet, she heard him gasp.

An impossible combination of pride and humility flooded her. She'd never felt so thoroughly a woman until now with Lee's gaze, as probing as a touch, sweeping over her.

As Lee's clothes fell one by one, Caitlin was astonished that anything masculine could be so sleekly perfect. She'd seen most of his dark, well-knit beauty before, but each time her brain, her whole body, absorbed the sexual shock wave anew. The fine muscles of his chest answered the movements of his arms as he pushed the last of his garments away from his hips. His quiet intensity left her breathless.

He walked slowly toward her. His thighs were magnificent, long and firmly muscled. Caitlin's heart was pouring hot blood into her arteries so fast she thought he must be able to see it pounding between her breasts. Lee's pulse was knocking in the strong, smooth column of his throat.

Lee didn't touch her. He let himself look and look and look. She was just as high as his heart. Everything about her was small; hands, feet, achingly exquisite breasts. She had no tan marks—no one as fair as Caitlin could tan—but the galaxies of freckles did end where the very white swells began.

He thought he could span her waist with his two hands. Not even the act of making love to her in the darkness had prepared him for the sight of this exciting, terrifying fragility. On one level, he wanted to crush her to him; on another, he was afraid of bruising that tender skin if he went too quickly.

"I love you," he said hoarsely. "I love you so."

He stood so close Caitlin could feel his arousal. Rising on tiptoe, she put her lips on his insistent pulse.

He pushed away tendrils of coppery hair so he could rest his thumbs on the pulse points just under her jaw. The thumbs gently rotated, massaging with infinite skill, until Caitlin moaned, wanting him to touch other, more urgent places. Lightly, inevitably, his knowing hands glided down to cup breasts aching for the pressure of his fingers, his mouth, his roving tongue. Her own hands desperately massaged his shoulders and back, slipping up to intertwine in the crisp hair at his nape and then down again to trace the line of his spine.

Only when he lifted his head did she realize she was being tumbled gently onto the bed. With maddening precision he set out to lave every part of her body.

At first, Caitlin wanted to giggle. But each methodical movement enticed her farther into a dreamlike state where nothing existed except the two of them in a world bounded by the corners of the massive bed. His very predictability gave her double pleasure; anticipation tingled in the nerve endings that preceded his touch, sensation burned in the wake of his mouth and tongue.

His delicate exploration reached a very private, already aroused place, and almost tipped her into fulfillment. He seemed to sense it. He pulled lightly and lovingly away to stretch full-length beside her.

Lee's loving had been special last night, but now he was remaking her into a mass of yearning. He took her beyond thought into a realm where it was natural to hear little, hungry animal sounds and not know which one of them was making them, to give and take and give with equal need.

Blindly, she reached out. Her hips tried to mold themselves to his. His hands traveled slowly from the sensitive skin of her waist till his palms were filled with the rounded undersides of her breasts and his fingers were firm under her pleading arms.

"Not so fast this time," he told her. "There's a lot about wanting I promised myself you were going to learn. It became an obsession around the time I took my hundredth cold shower. Last night we went way, way too quickly. Today we don't hurry."

Caitlin almost sobbed, "You started teaching me about wanting when you kept me from falling that first day, remember? You held me and nothing had ever felt that good. Oh, please, damn, now, hurry, Lee—"

His laugh was a deep, pleased rumble. "Okay, okay, but let's go slow, sweetheart. Be soft for me."

She went limp with love. He applied protection, as light and shade from reflected water danced across the ceiling and rippled over them. In the fugitive caress of sun and shadow, he swung her effortlessly above him and, stroke by stroke, lowered her until they were joined completely.

The rhythm they set together was smooth and seductive, steadier than Caitlin's heartbeat, but each thrust Lee made found her hidden spring and wound it up a little farther.

The only sound in the world was their mingled breath. When Lee's fingertips slid back to linger on her breasts, Caitlin gasped, "Oh, love! Love, love . . ."

Somehow what he was doing to the rosy tips heated the coil, making it vibrate with undischarged tension. She tried to shiver closer.

Her love words broke his iron control, and he surged into a demanding drumbeat that shook a full-fledged sob from her as the coil, tightened unbearably, sprang into release, creating intense flashes of pure pleasure.

It was like trying to contain her own small, personal lightning storm. A stifled scream escaped her at the surprise of it. Her cry triggered the thunder of Lee's climax.

Spent at last, they rocked gently to a stop. Their eyes, hazel and blue, studied each other in exhausted wonder. Caitlin kissed away the tiny salt drops that beaded his upper lip.

It hurt—not physically, but in a real sense—to slip away from him. Caitlin whispered, "Oh, love," again, and Lee pulled her to rest in his arms.

It felt so comfortable there that she gradually relaxed into sleep.

She didn't know what woke her. One moment she was pleasurably asleep, the next pleasurably awake. She didn't need to turn her head to see Lee, who lay tidily, with one arm still pillowing her neck. Sleep softened the decided personality that made his extraordinary handsomeness human in waking. What remained looked younger, heart-stoppingly beautiful in an idealized, Renaissance way. Like a sketch by Leonardo. But it wasn't her Lee. At least, not all of him.

More than just a pretty face, she thought.

Happiness rippled through her, causing her to curl closer to the source of her joy. Lee blinked, then his whole body galvanized into an enormous stretch that ended with his big arms engulfing her.

"Hello," he growled in her ear, which he caught briefly between his teeth. "I remember you."

Caitlin dissolved into laughter. "I certainly hope so. I presume I'm the last thing you saw before you most ungallantly took a nap."

"Ah, that's where I've seen you before. No wonder you seem familiar. And as to naps—"

"Speaking of familiar," interrupted Caitlin, "would you like to take a shower with me?"

Along with the usual facilities, the bathroom contained a large square stall adorned with a complicated shower head and a series of mysterious knobs and buttons.

"Good heavens, what's this?" Caitlin asked, poking one at random.

Mist seeped toward them through a vent near the floor.

"I think you're going to get a sauna," said Lee.

The frosted glass doors were already shut. Caitlin observed a shelf, tiled in nile green, jutting out at knee height. She shook her tousled halo at Lee in mock panic. "But I don't like saunas!"

Lee's eyes were very alive in his narrow face. "That's because you've never taken one with me."

His mouth on hers was tentative and searching, as if it hadn't known all of her so well a short while ago. The sweet, timeless kiss seemed to last forever, until Lee murmured, "Caitlin? Honey? Can you give me more?"

A quick touch of his tongue hinted at what he wanted. But she'd never loved a man in that particular way before. The idea didn't shock, and yet it raised specters from her past. A tremor ran through her straight to her feet, caused by fear. Fear that, despite Lee's easily seen satisfaction with all their lovemaking, she really wasn't woman enough, seductress enough, sexy enough, to be the aggressor in a game he was expert at and she wasn't. She feared failing, again, to hold a man.

The fog loomed waist-high, and a fine sweat broke out over Caitlin's body. Lee, too, was acquiring a glossy sheen, but perspiration added a bronze gleam to his smooth skin that made her want to touch. The thought came to her sharply that Lee was also naked, all his secrets bare for her to discover, and he wasn't afraid.

She parted her lips. Slowly and thoroughly, she began to experiment with the hard planes of his chest, softened only by the frenetic pulse of his heart and the downy covering that formed a wedge descending to his flat midriff. At first she felt awkward, untested. Then self-consciousness became lost in sensation. *Black silk,* she thought, as her sensitized lips followed the V of springy hair to its base. She tasted and teased, and though he was fully aroused she couldn't resist tantalizing him even more. His hands came out of the hot white mist and guided her to where her mouth pleased him most.

Her body felt like a candle, her tongue a flame that flickered and weaved and lit an answering spark wherever it went.

With a slight pressure he rotated her eager mouth away from his flesh so he could lift her onto the wide bench. Caitlin was both amused and moved to see that he'd brought protection with him.

"Come here, cat eyes." He spoke in a low bass that excited her intensely. Superheated water vapor formed a semitransparent cloud, filling the chamber. Humidity forced her to take shallow breaths that left her light-headed. She thought perhaps it was Lee, not the sauna, making her senses swim. A thousand pressure points craved the moisture-laden friction of his body. *"Lee..."*

"Caitie, you're velvet. Let me feel you—"

Her need met his to complete their union. Lee gasped as she arched with fierce urgency to help make them one. Her legs gripped him, locking him close. She pulled his head down so she could quench the heat of her lips against the moistness of his mouth, but the thirsty kisses only enflamed her further.

Her center felt consumed by elemental need, striving again and again to experience him fully. The demand between them blazed hotter and higher. It spun out of control inside her and then spread and eddied until her whole body was suffused by a warming glow.

Lee's passion accelerated and, incredibly, kindled the coals of her desire so she shared the strong shudders that left him spent and panting in her arms.

It could have been a minute or an hour later that he carefully set her upright.

Caitlin pushed back the auburn tendrils clinging to her cheeks. "I feel vaporized."

"Well, no wonder."

"Oh, Lee, I wasn't talking about the Turkish bath."

Steam dissipated to show her his strong teeth flashing.

"Let's try to figure out these rocket controls so we can have a shower," he said.

"No, thank you. I tried having a nice, uncomplicated shower with you already."

"Ah, but you can trust me this time. I'm hungry. And," he said as he adjusted the fine spray, "I intend to eat some food before we come back here for dessert."

12

CAITLIN WAS SURPRISED to hear Lee declare it was too late for lunch and too early for supper.

"Says who?" she demanded. "Lee, it's been months since breakfast. I'm fading away."

"Don't do that." His fingers linked with hers. "I'll feed you, I promise. I could use a little nourishment myself, remember. Healthy exercise takes a lot out of a guy. But I noticed a shop when I registered. . . ."

A pinprick of disappointment made the tiniest possible puncture in Caitlin's contentment. Making detailed observations of the hotel's amenities had been the last thing on her mind earlier in the day. Somehow it struck her as less than romantic that Lee had been detached enough to pay attention to irrelevancies. Men were different, she reminded herself.

Thinking about the ways in which Lee was different erased the pucker from between her brows.

There were, in fact, several small, consciously expensive shops clustered near the lobby. Caitlin glanced idly at the precisely arranged disorder of an art gallery and said, "My, this place does have pretensions, doesn't it?"

"Not quite as rustic as I'd imagined northern Idaho," Lee agreed absently, and steered her toward another entrance. "In here."

It was a jewelry store.

Caitlin forgot her rumbling stomach. "I misjudged you," she murmured as they walked, hand in hand, to the counter.

"Did you, sweetheart?"

"Yes, I was mad—not mad, exactly, a little hurt—because you were busy checking out the consumer goods when it was all I could do not to pull you down behind the potted plants."

A middle-aged woman, hair and smile lacquered into place, approached and instantly fell prey to Lee's warm laughter. "We'd like to see a really large, gaudy diamond," he told her.

As the salesclerk scurried to comply, Lee explained, "I was on the lookout for someplace to buy a ring, so I could put my claim on you as fast and as publicly as possible. You'll note, however, that I kept my priorities straight," he added with a look that made her flush to the roots of her hair. "We didn't go shopping absolutely as soon as possible."

"That seems to be my recollection, too." She met his eyes and felt herself drowning in blue. "Lee, unless you're set on decking me out in diamonds, I think I'd prefer a sapphire."

They compromised on a star sapphire surrounded by diamonds in an antique gold setting. It fit her slender finger perfectly.

With Lee's ring conspicuous on her hand, Caitlin felt dressed up. A good thing, too, she thought. Her overnight bag contained a toothbrush and the startlingly abbreviated cobalt silk nightgown that she might or might not have a chance to model for him later. Her suspicion that she had underpacked for dinner at a hotel with fancy bathrooms was confirmed the minute they entered the dining room.

Casual attire had been abandoned by the other guests in favor of more formal dress. At any other time, she would have been embarrassed. Her raglan-sleeved sage-green cardigan and matching slacks had been rescued from the floor uncreased but were woefully inadequate next to the profusion of sequins and puffs on display. Tonight it didn't matter. With Lee's appreciative glance on her and the star in the engagement ring he'd given her flashing milkily from its sapphire depths, Caitlin knew she didn't have to compete.

"That color suits you," he said, as the waiter, rather like a magician, flourished the menus before allowing them to be examined.

Caitlin smiled. "I was more or less ramrodded into buying it. The outfit, I mean, not the ring." She put an inquisitive finger to the side of her head. "My hair's still wet."

"That suits you, too." He grinned crookedly. "Mahogany streaks instead of copper spangles."

His tender gaze was impossible to sustain. Caitlin took refuge in her menu.

"L-lee, look at this! There aren't any prices!"

Lee ran an eye disinterestedly over the columns. "There aren't, are there? Don't worry, it won't bust the bank if you order whatever appeals to you."

"Well, thank you, but this ring cost a mint and—criminy, don't you want to know what they're going to charge?"

"Have no fear. It'll show up on the bill." His grin widened. "In case you're concerned, I did all right out of my contract with the pros, and had some luck investing. The conference pays me a reasonable salary. We won't be rich, you understand, but comfortable. If I could have brought myself to do deodorant commercials when I was still marginally famous, you could have been marrying real money."

The waiter chose that moment to reappear. After he retired with their orders, Caitlin studied Lee. Leaning back in his chair, he was at home here as he was on the Tall Pines campus, or at the lake, or alone with her. It wasn't a facade. He was simply, naturally, himself with no need to impress others.

A nagging insecurity led her to ask, "It doesn't faze you, does it? I mean, this morning you were roughing it at what Auretta, not without justice, calls my shack—"

"I can just hear her saying it."

"Uh-huh. And now we're here." Her upturned palm included the carefully flattering lights, dainty tables and small army of waiters, as well as the famous couple she'd seen earlier in the lobby. "But the comparison doesn't bother you."

"Comparisons are odious," he quoted offhandedly.

"Yes, but most people can't help making them. I guess I'm trying to say I admire your self-assurance."

Lee picked up and put down a piece of the staggering array of cutlery that flanked his plate. Self-assurance? he thought. On the contrary, his nerves were stretched to the breaking point.

From the moment he'd put the ring on her finger, he'd felt like a louse. There was something about the act, symbolic as it was, that made their relationship formal, a game with rules. And one of the rules was a man didn't prepare to marry a woman and remain less than truthful with her. Especially not a woman like Caitlin, whose lovemaking was so wholehearted and generous it left him ashamed he hadn't been open with her already. However she reacted, he had to tell her about Jim.

"That leads to a subject I've been meaning to talk to you about."

"Something nice?"

"No. Something rather grim, in fact. I was hoping—but you've got to know sooner or later," he argued with himself.

"Okay," she said placidly. "You have my permission to continue."

He took both her hands in a hard grasp. "God, I hate hurting you," he muttered.

"Well, then, don't." She instantly shook her head. "I didn't mean that. If there's something you need to tell me, just—tell me. Don't try to keep it inside."

He gave her hands an extra squeeze before he let them go. "All right," he began. "It's—"

"Oh oh," broke in Caitlin. "We've been spotted."

"So?"

"So it's the busiest busybody I know and she's headed this way, looking for dirt."

The acquaintance divided her attention between Lee and Caitlin's sapphire. After several gushing references to its size and probable cost, she said, "I'm on my way to the little girls' room, and I never like to go by myself. Caitlin, dear, would you?"

Thinking it would be the quickest way to get rid of this pest, Caitlin rose, smiled apologetically at Lee and followed her.

Ensconced in front of the wide mirror in the ladies' lounge, Caitlin underwent a battery of questions she almost wished Lee could hear. It would be fun to compare notes with a professional about the woman's interrogation technique. She tried to confine her answers to yes, no and maybe, but when the prying progressed from Lee's career and financial status to "I don't know, he looks like a male model to me. Are you sure he's not gay?" she replied icily, "Yes, thank you, positively sure."

Then she was sorry, because her inquisitor's eyes darted to her face, and Caitlin could see in the reflection that her lips looked full and pouting and kissed. She decided enough was enough. The woman's curiosity was avid and distasteful, and Caitlin had more important things to attend to. Like Lee.

"Excuse me, but I'd better be going, in case my fiancé's tempted to run off with the headwaiter."

She reseated herself opposite Lee with a little flounce. "I feel smirched," she commented.

Caitlin expected Lee's somber air to lighten, and it did, but for once his smile seemed forced. "Anything I can do about it?" he asked.

"Maybe later." What was the matter with her? she wondered. By rights, this should be one of the best evenings of her life, and she was spoiling it by surrendering to piddling little irritations. Could it be her subconscious, rebelling against the happiness it was always reminding her she didn't deserve?

She peeked over at Lee and concern for him swamped her self-analysis. He was actually fidgeting. She couldn't remember him ever wasting a motion before. Her mood must have communicated itself to him.

Repentant, she said with determined cheerfulness, "In fact, I was hoping you might want to kiss and make it better."

The blue devils in his eyes seemed to have gone out. "Caitie, I have to talk to you about the job I've been doing."

So that was it. Caitlin relaxed. Lee was nothing like Jim, but perhaps there were some things about men, even the nicest of them, that were universal. If there was one marital duty she had sufficient practice in, it was listening while her man told her about work.

"I hope it's going well. Have you caught all the crooks or the perpetrators or whatever you investigators call them?"

Lee said slowly, "The boosters responsible for the trouble at TPU aren't crooks. They haven't broken any laws. Keep that in mind, Cait."

"Granted," she allowed. "But if teaching young people that everything's for sale and they should put themselves up to the highest bidder isn't illegal, it ought to be."

"Be that as it may, all I'm called on to do is pinpoint the rah-rah boys and confirm for the conference that they're no longer associated with Tall Pines. Silverthorne started that process before I ever arrived. The problem's almost solved. When it is, it'll be time for me to move on. To Seattle, if I get kicked upstairs."

"You dumb jock," she said very softly. "Don't you know yet I'd live with you anywhere?" As she spoke, she was thinking of the opening she had applied for within Lee's organization. If that didn't pan out, there would be other possibilities in public, school, medical, even corporate libraries. Seattle was a big city; she'd find something. Should Lee's promotion fall through for some unfathomable reason, her skills would be marketable anywhere. Even if it took a while, Lee was all the security she'd ever need. Suddenly job hunting felt like an adventure.

He started to speak, but just then the waiter reappeared with a soup tureen carved out of a large real pumpkin. He set this in the middle of the table with a reverent air, and placed tiny pumpkins shaped into bowls in front of each of them. He seemed to be waiting for applause. When Lee merely flicked his hand impatiently, the man looked offended and ladled liquid into the artfully carved dishes rather listlessly, Caitlin thought. A brown splash marred the impeccable peach tablecloth.

He renewed the champagne in their glasses with more care. Caitlin raised her napkin to her mouth to hide her smile. It always amused her to see restaurant employees treat wine as if they were devotees at the altar of Bacchus. Encrusted with ribbons and labels, this bottle really did warrant respect. The champagne was good, too.

Lee waited until the waiter whisked himself off to say gently, "You take my breath away. But Cait, there was a reason why I wanted to get you away for this weekend."

She stopped spooning up her soup to stare at him. "I wonder what that could have been."

"Not what you're thinking, I'm afraid. At least, not entirely, although I certainly don't have any complaints to make about that part of the trip."

"Thank you, sir, for those kind words. It's nice to know I can always go to you for a recommendation."

He was still looking too serious. Caitlin slipped one foot out of a moccasin and slyly inserted her toes into a leg of Lee's pants. Her toes curled and rubbed with a catlike instinct for the voluptuous. "This is delicious soup. I've never had pumpkin before. What do you suppose they used to season it?"

"I haven't got the faintest idea," he said in exasperation. "Will you cut that out? It's interfering with my concentration."

"Good. That's what I hoped it would do."

"Some old maid librarian you turned out to be."

"I've never pretended to be an old maid with you." She withdrew her foot. It felt cold removed from Lee's flesh. "Is that what's bothering you? The fact that I used to be married to Jim?"

"Oh, Caitie." He drummed a spoon against the side of his pumpkin. It made a muted thud, causing her to realize he hadn't been drinking his soup. "No. Haven't I shown you that that couldn't matter less to me?"

She patted the floor with her bare foot, trying to locate her missing shoe. "That's certainly what I inferred from your behavior. Among other things. Don't you love to throw 'infer' into conversations, just to show you know it doesn't mean 'imply'? Can you feel my shoe over on your side? It seems to have gone missing."

Lee peered under the table. "It's under your chair, to the right. Sweetheart, you could have been married a hundred times—okay, maybe not a hundred, I might begin to wonder how you got rid of your excess husbands—but you're right in a way. It is Jim I need to talk to you about."

Caitlin pushed her empty bowl to one side and folded her hands on the table. "What about Jim?"

Sympathy blocked the words he'd rehearsed while she was in the rest room. Caitlin looked so unsuspecting. With her fingers primly intertwined, she could have been a schoolgirl, except that her face was pink and her eyes heavy-lidded, her lips red and swollen from loving. *I hate this*, he thought, but he had to go on. Even if he wanted to keep secrets from Caitlin, there was every possibility that an aftershock to the scandal that had rocked Tall Pines could hit any day. The original letters could surface at any time, and he feared Caitlin would never trust him again if he allowed her to hear about them from someone else.

But how would he handle the failure if he brought the blank wretchedness back to her eyes and couldn't banish it again?

Carefully he said, "You know the Mallorys."

"Of course I know the Mallorys. I've lived next door to them for three years."

"Ed Mallory is closely connected to the violations at Tall Pines."

Caitlin smacked the table with her clenched hands. "I knew it! He's always tried to cultivate me in this weird sort of way. What is he, the ringleader?"

"'Fraid not," Lee replied. "Honey, he's the person who went to the conference officials in the first place. He's been hanging around you to see if you'd let something slip."

"Let something—what's that supposed to mean?"

Candlelight wavered on Lee's features. One moment the curve of his cheek stood out; the next it lapsed into shadow. It was the face of a stranger.

"It means he claims to have notes in Jim's handwriting to a couple of fans, types Silverthorne's booted out

of the official boosters' club. Apparently it's pretty clear
from them that Jim was aware of what the zealots were
up to."

"No."

The single syllable was quiet and flat, but Lee's eye-
brows snapped together.

"Unfortunately, it's yes. The fancy vacations, the
nonexistent jobs, cars, girls...you name it. If Mallory's
not pulling a fast one—and I can't imagine why he
would—Jim didn't participate actively in the corruption, but he did know and never did a thing to stop it."

"Lee, don't say this."

"Do you think I'm enjoying it?" Anguish for her
made him harsh. "Recruiting for college ball can be
cutthroat. Alumni like winning teams. The pressure on
Jim to produce must have been tremendous. He
couldn't do that without quality players. So the boosters went out and bought him some."

"I'd have known. Maybe the marriage wasn't as—as
close as it should have been, but we loved each other.
It's taken me a long time to let go. Part of me still feels
guilty that I'm alive and happy and with you. Don't
make me defend Jim to you."

"Caitlin, you don't have to."

"Yes, I do. Jim was a decent man. He loved those
players as much as—maybe more than—he loved me.
He would never have stood by and let them be—be de-
graded. If he were that kind of person, I'd have known
it, dammit."

"But you didn't. I believe that like I believe in the sun
rising tomorrow. Don't you see how it could have been?
He protected you from what was happening. He
wouldn't have wanted you tainted. Any decent man

would cherish your honesty." He broke off. "Don't look like that, Cait. Nobody could doubt he loved you very much."

Caitlin felt the way she had that night at the pool—drowning, helpless. Only this time Lee wasn't coming to her rescue. He was pulling her down, back into the old black morass of confusion and loneliness. Well, she'd struggled out of it before on her own. She could do it again.

A warming rush of anger returned strength to Caitlin's vocal cords. "Please refrain from giving me your speculation about my marriage. You've just accused my husband of being a cheat."

Her wide, unblinking stare was filled with the implacable hatred of a wildcat. Controlling his own rising temper, Lee said, "What I said was he probably knew cheating was going on." It didn't seem to be the moment to point out that Jim, by virtue of the till-death-us-do-part clause in the wedding vows, was no longer Caitlin's husband, or that it was his own ring she was wearing on her left hand.

"You're a liar. You brought me here to soften me up. Did you think all you had to do was take me to bed a few times and I'd be so—so overcome with love I'd let you get away with this?"

The color seeped away from Lee's face, leaving it as beautiful and as lifeless as marble. "Caitlin, for God's sake, you have to know better than that."

"Do I? Why? Because the great Lee Michaels says so? Just what are you hiding? Or should I say whom? Who's paying you?"

"I'm not even going to respond to that."

Waiters were converging on their table as the other diners sat rapt but Caitlin ignored them. All her attention was focused on Lee, who she had thought loved her. The table bucked when she suddenly stood up. Her pumpkin teetered over the edge and fell with a soggy plop. Caitlin grabbed the errant moccasin and slammed it on her foot, not caring how ridiculous she looked.

"Of course not," she said contemptuously. "But I'll tell you something, hotshot investigator. Consider it a promise. I'll find out who you're really working for and why that person wants you to smear Jim. And when I have proof, I'm going to break you."

Wrenching the ring from her finger, she dropped it on the table. The glittering circle bounced once and splashed into Lee's champagne glass.

Two functionaries oozed up and tried to take Caitlin's arms. She simply looked at them. "Don't you dare," she said. Sweeping up her purse, head high, she walked out of the room.

13

"WHAT DOES IT COST for half a room for one day?" Caitlin asked the desk clerk.

The young woman looked alarmed. "That's not how we rent rooms. You need somebody to share accommodations with if you only want to pay half price."

"That's not my problem. I want to pay what I owe for a room I'm checking out of. The other person who was using the room will pay for his half later."

"Oh. I'm not sure . . . I'll have to ask. . . ."

Caitlin said bluntly, "If you're worried this is some sort of scam to get out of half the bill, you're wrong. You can see in your records there were two of us registered. It's just that I'm leaving separately from—the other occupant—and I don't particularly want to run into him again."

Ever again, she thought.

"Yeah." The girl cheered up, as if this part at least was comprehensible. "I've had dates like that. The creep made you go Dutch, huh?"

Caitlin was too honest to confirm the assumption and too angry to deny it. The clerk didn't seem to expect any reply.

"I s'pose it's okay. Let's see, that comes to . . ."

It was a staggering amount, especially considering it was only half the total and didn't include her uneaten dinner, but Caitlin pulled out her credit card.

"I also need some way to get to Spokane tonight. I don't have my car."

The receptionist tucked the credit slip into a drawer. "That's a tough one. This isn't exactly a metropolis, you know. The rental car place is closed for the night. I don't s'pose—how much do you want to get away from this guy?"

Caitlin searched in her purse for cash. It disappeared into another drawer.

"The guy who picks up the laundry usually sticks around to scrounge supper. Maybe he can help you out. If you don't mind riding in the front of a laundry truck."

At that point, Caitlin wouldn't have balked at riding in the back of a laundry truck.

"Could you hurry, please?" She was watching the entrance to the dining room. "I just want to go home."

Within a few minutes, the clerk reported that the driver was willing to oblige. Lee didn't appear.

The ride to the city was silent. As the truck jolted along the dark highway, Caitlin thought that Cinderella's pumpkin was shattered once and for all. No more glass slipper time. It was back to the solitary workaday world for her.

The last of her cash went to the laundryman, who accepted it without a word and drove off in a clash of gears. Mercifully, the convenience store where he'd dropped her had a working telephone from which she called a taxi.

The cab took half an hour to arrive. When it did, exhaustion settled into her bones as she sank as far as she was able into the cracked vinyl seating. She spent the fifteen minute trip staring out the window and seeing nothing.

The cabbie, too, was uncommunicative, leaving Caitlin alone with her thoughts. They swirled in a misery of confusion. The only clear image was the memory of Lee's face as she spit out her rejection. All the power and vibrant life had drained away, as if she'd killed him and he didn't realize yet he was supposed to stop breathing.

Caitlin told herself fiercely to stop imagining she could fathom Lee's emotions. His attraction to her, his practiced lovemaking had been an elaborate charade, proven by his slander against Jim. It must all be part of an act to persuade her to accept Ed Mallory's bizarre accusation. Why else would Lee believe Ed instead of her?

Jim would never have condoned anything but good sportsmanship in the game he loved. His integrity was as predictable as the sun's rising and setting.

Someone had said almost those same words to her today. When she remembered it was Lee, the tears she'd suppressed for hours began to run down her cheeks and drip, unchecked, into her lap. How could he believe Ed Mallory?

Finally the taxi crunched over the harvest of windblown leaves to halt at her house. Caitlin scrawled a barely recognizable signature across a check.

"Hey, lady, the boss isn't going to like this."

"Take it or leave it," she told him wearily. "There's no money in the house."

He shrugged and took it. She plodded up the path to the porch. She didn't know how long it took her to insert her key into the lock. A long time.

She pulled herself up the stairs like an old lady. No kamikaze fur ball hurtled itself in greeting under her feet, and after a while, she recalled that Flame was with Auretta. She wouldn't even have the comfort of her pet in bed with her.

Caitlin was definitely sleeping alone tonight.

AT AURETTA'S the next morning, Auretta surveyed her critically. "You look terrible."

Caitlin scooped up Flame. "I didn't get much sleep," she said noncommittally.

"That sounds encouraging," responded Auretta, pushing a mugful of coffee toward her. "Neither did I," she added happily. "Curly didn't leave till two in the morning. I practically had to put him out with the milk bottles."

"Curly?" Caitlin had the distinct recollection the physics professor was bald as an egg.

"Yes, Curly. He didn't talk boring old science last night," said Auretta smugly.

Caitlin put Flame in her lap, where the cat immediately closed her eyes and started purring so frantically the small body rocked from side to side. Caitlin tasted the coffee. Auretta had made it hot and black, but somehow the caffeine wasn't cheering.

"So how did everything work out with you and Lee?"

"It didn't," Caitlin said. "That is, it did at first, but then—it just didn't, that's all. I doubt I'll be seeing him again."

Auretta's round face creased in distress. "A fight?"

"Not exactly. More like a nuclear explosion. I lost my temper."

"Child, that's ridiculous. You don't have a temper. Time and again I've wished you could get more het up about things."

Caitlin scratched Flame under the chin. "Trust me. I got het up."

"Lee's not the argumentative type. Maybe you can make up."

"Let's talk about something else, okay?"

"Oh, all right," Auretta grumbled. "But if you ever need to unburden yourself, you come right to me. I'm dying to hear all about it. And I still think you could—"

"Did Flame behave herself?" Caitlin asked in a desperate voice.

"I'll just tell you what that junior mountain lion tried to do...."

They tricked the cat into the cage with a catnip mouse. Caitlin talked consoling nothings all the way home, pretending to herself it was to keep Flame from yowling. Really, she hoped the effort of stringing words together would smother her own dreary thoughts.

Once she'd released her pet into the house, she forced herself to finish a series of minor chores with the same goal in mind. But paying bills and vacuuming already-clean rugs took far too little time. When she found herself in the kitchen contemplating an overhaul of the spice cabinet, she admitted defeat. All she could think of was Lee.

Library science didn't call for much math, but it did require logic. The problem confronting Caitlin resolved into a nasty little equation. Lee said Jim condoned fraud. Caitlin knew Jim had been honest. Therefore, Lee was lying. But why? In her heart, she knew Lee couldn't be bribed. Why would anyone even want to? So was it the promotion? But Lee had never seemed to be driven by ambition....

Caitlin sat at the kitchen table with this reasoning circling endlessly through her brain. After a while, a door slammed and Toby skidded to a halt in front of the refrigerator.

"So here you are," he said, upending a half gallon of milk and drinking directly from the carton. Caitlin didn't bother to scold. Let Brenda worry about such details. There were other subjects to discuss.

Before she could begin, Toby said, "There's some stuff we have to get cleared away."

She furrowed her brow. Her brain was so tired of thinking. "I'm sorry, Toby, what are you talking about?"

Toby looked down at her. He was so tall—taller than his father, only an inch or two short of Lee's considerable height. When had Toby grown into this formidable physical specimen?

"I'm talking about you and me, Ma. This is family stuff."

Auretta and Lee were right. Toby wasn't just on the threshold of manhood, he was bursting into it. Well, he'd need all the maturity he could muster to weather the lies Lee was going to voice against his father.

Toby said, "Lee called Brenda's folks about five this morning to find out if you were at their cabin. Since you weren't, we picked him up before dawn and went to see if you were at our place instead."

"How could I have gotten there? No boat, stupid."

"Lee didn't say so, but I got the feeling he was afraid you were so mad about something you might have stolen one."

Caitlin could think of nothing to say except, "Well, I didn't. I was here."

"Yeah, but nobody knew that because the phone was off the hook." He picked up the receiver and replaced it. "The operator couldn't tell if it was broken or what."

Flushing, she explained, "I didn't want to talk to—anyone."

"I guess not. Look, I don't know what went wrong between you and Lee yesterday, and you don't need to say it's none of my business because I'm not asking. I'm sorry for it, that's all."

Caitlin simply nodded.

"I hope the fact you and Lee had a fight—"

"Worse than a fight," she said painfully.

"Okay, I'm sorry about that, too. Brenda and I thought you two were good together. But, listen, I'm not butting in. The thing is, this sort of complicates my plans, and Ma, I couldn't stand to hurt you."

This was the second time in two days one of the men in her life had declared his reluctance to wound her, she thought with mordant humor. What could Toby possibly do to her? She already felt like the walking dead.

"Okay, bud, spill the beans."

The milk carton was still in his hands. It made an absurd popping noise when his big fingers flexed around it. With a start, he put it down on the counter. A slow flush rose from his neck to his shock of sandy hair. Whatever was upsetting him couldn't be as bad as her news, but she said gently, "Is it so awful?"

"Actually, I'm kind of hyped about it."

"Toby, could you please get to the point?"

"Yeah, the point. The point is I'm going to try out for football my sophomore year. There'll be a new coach, but everybody says I'll be a shoo-in for offense. Of course, this season's going to be pretty much a write-off. We're not going to win anything. I took Bren to the game last week and it was a massacre. But the staff's all excited about building for next year."

Caitlin was completely baffled. "What's this got to do with Lee?"

"Nothing. Except that he said something to me—you remember—when we were at the lake. He asked if I could throw a ball. Well, I can. And I can catch one and I can run. Dad used to work with me a lot, and he always said I could be good. I guess I just want the chance to find out."

She shook her head to clear it of the echo of Lee's voice. He'd said that, too. Was she going to spend the rest of her life remembering things Lee had said?

"I've never tried to keep you from playing football, Toby."

He shrugged. "It was obvious you hated it. I mean, you haven't been to a TPU game in three years. We used to go all the time. You blame football for killing Dad."

Flame trotted through the room and out the pet door onto the back porch. The little wooden flap swung back and forth on its hinges.

"You'd better let her out," Caitlin said.

She watched Toby cross the floor. He had an economy of movement, a natural grace, which she hadn't noticed before. If he could transfer that precision to the gridiron, there was no doubt he'd be an asset to Tall Pines on the scrimmage line.

"I didn't blame football for Jim's death," Caitlin said. "It absorbed him to the exclusion of everything else. I was jealous, that's all. I certainly never meant to discourage you from trying out for the team if that's what you want. It should have occurred to me you'd have an aptitude. After all, I saw Jim practicing with you out on the field often enough. But later you didn't say anything, and I was too blind to ask."

Toby touched her shoulder. "I knew deep down if I said anything you wouldn't make a fuss. Lee said so, too."

"Oh, did he? And when was this?"

Toby screwed up his face in apology. "We got together a few times. We, uh, sort of mapped a strategy for breaking the news to you. He more or less said you and I have been underestimating each other and it was time we freed each other to act like adults. And he told me you'd be horrified if you ever found out I was giving up football to spare your feelings."

"He was right about that, damn him," Caitlin admitted. "Toby, I'm so sorry. I've been every bit as manipulative as he has."

"You mean Lee?" Toby asked. "Lee's not—"

"Never mind. You like him, don't you?"

Toby looked at her steadily. "A lot."

Caitlin licked her lips. "Toby, Lee isn't really our friend. He's going to make some claims—some terrible claims about Jim. It's impossible, but Lee says letters Jim wrote years ago prove that your dad knew about the violations in the recruiting program."

Toby's youthful face closed so she couldn't read his expression.

"Letters? Dad wrote letters?"

"No, of course not. They're forgeries—if they exist at all. They must be."

"Not necessarily."

Caitlin stared. "Not— Toby, what are you talking about?"

He swore softly and at great length. Toby, who never swore. A day earlier, she would have been shocked, might have said something pointed about his language. Now she waited wide-eyed until he finished. Toby couldn't mean what "not necessarily" sounded like. *Please, God. How many times can the world fall apart in the space of twenty-four hours?*

She said, "You'd better explain what's going on."

"How much do you know?"

She shook her head helplessly.

"Ma, don't look like that. I mean, it's bad but it's *over*. Dad's dead. He can't lose his job because of this." Toby tried to grin. "I know, I'm not funny. But when you think about it, that's what would have bugged him the most if he'd been found out while he was still alive. Losing his coaching job."

Caitlin's heart stopped beating. When it started again, the rush of blood was so agonizing she crossed her arms over her chest. "You're saying he knew about the violations. Bribing the players with money. *Pandering*."

He shot her a harassed look. "Yeah."

"Toby, it's just not possible."

"Do you think I like it?" he exploded. "Can you imagine how I've felt watching Lee dig around in the files, talk to Dad's old friends and *know* that if he dug long enough he'd find some dirt?" He used another short, ugly word. "Ma, I like Lee. He's a great guy. I almost— I almost sat down and talked to him about the whole mess." He said it in a rush, as if admitting a weakness.

Slowly Caitlin's mind began to function again. "Maybe you should have."

He laughed without mirth. "And told him what? That my dad was up to his neck in recruiting violations? What would that have made me? I couldn't turn in my own father."

"No, of course not," she agreed.

Poor Toby. She writhed inwardly. For three years she'd tried to deny he was growing up, and all the while he'd carried this adult burden of knowledge by himself. "When did you find out about—" She couldn't say it.

He shrugged. "That's like asking when did I first hold a football. Dad let me hang around the field house all the time. It's not like it was any big secret among the players. They talked about it to one another. Who got paid for jobs they didn't have to show up for, which cheerleaders would keep the incoming freshmen happy if they signed with TPU." He colored. "It seemed like the normal way things got done. But after you married Dad, I started to look at everything differently."

"But I never knew—"

"Yeah, but here you were, this big fan. I could tell you worshiped Dad, and yet you never allowed much slack where honesty was concerned. And then . . ."

"And then?" she prompted gently.

"Dad took me aside—man to man. He said that players were special, that they deserved what he called 'special incentives' and they followed rules that ordinary people couldn't understand. We were never supposed to talk about it. Especially to you. I guess he knew you wouldn't take it very well. It took me a long time to work out the way Dad thought. He didn't see what he was letting happen as wrong. They were just things that had to be done if TPU was going to compete in the big time."

"The big time is relative," she said, thinking of Lee and his shattered pro career. He'd given up his place in the spotlight without whimpering. Or cheating.

"Dad liked to win," said Toby.

"The cost was too high." She looked at Jim's son fearfully. "You think the cost was too high, don't you, Toby?"

"Are you asking what I'd have done in the same situation? I've thought about it a lot. I'd try to make the players and the boosters stop. If there wasn't any way to keep them from doing it and still hang on to my job, I'd blow the whistle and quit. Football's supposed to be fun, not some big life-and-death issue. But I don't love Dad any less because he called it differently. Do you?"

Caitlin didn't answer.

Toby's mouth fell open in dawning horror. "Ma, is this why you and Lee broke up? Why you came home early?"

Caitlin stood and brushed aside the muslin curtains that hung so prettily at the window. Flame was an orange-and-white puddle on the hood of the car.

"Ma, you've got to tell him, explain—"

Caitlin didn't turn around. "It doesn't matter. He'll never speak to me again."

14

CAITLIN PUT her index finger on the doorbell and kept it there until Ed Mallory answered the door.

She could hardly believe this ghastly day had progressed only as far as lunchtime, but Ed had a frosting of crumbs on his chin. Caitlin didn't apologize. She said, "I hear you've got some letters written by my husband."

He passed a hand over the bottom of his face. "You'd better come in. We can't talk about this outside."

She trailed him into the living room and sat in the uncomfortably overstuffed chair he indicated, but continued on the attack. "What do those letter say, Ed?"

He eyed her shrewdly. "I think you know what they say."

For the first time, she could see the smart judgment that made Ed a successful businessman. "If I do," she said, "then you ought to agree that I have an interest in what you plan to do with them."

His full lips pursed. "Maybe so. Maybe not."

Caitlin kept a tight rein on her temper. Losing it had already cost her more than she could bear to contemplate.

"Ed, I'm aware that I don't have a right—legal or any other sort—to tell you what to do. But from what I've heard, I've gotten the impression you'd like to get the program cleaned up without implicating Jim."

"He was a good man," said Ed gruffly. "The recruitment stuff, I don't know. I kept my mouth shut a lot of years because I thought if Jim didn't see anything wrong with it . . . Finally the taste in my mouth just got so bad I had to spit it out. But I never dreamed Michaels would go after Jim."

"It's important to his career," she explained in a neutral voice. "Besides, Lee isn't a halfway sort of person. Once he makes up his mind about what he wants, he doesn't change it."

Although after her outburst, she thought, Lee couldn't possibly want her any longer. And he might occasionally moderate his tactics to fit changing circumstances. She remembered magic and electric blankets.

With her next words, her voice shook. "I'm wandering from the subject. Ed, I think you've been a great friend to Jim, better than he deserved in this case. You've certainly behaved with great sensitivity during the investigation."

He turned beet red, as if sensitivity were a particularly nasty perversion she was accusing him of committing. "You can butter me up all you want to. I'm not giving you those letters, and that's flat."

Well, she thought, Lee had warned her of how Ed regarded her.

"Fine. I'm not asking for the letters." She didn't want to touch them, if the truth were told. The very idea Jim had written them made her long for a hot shower, though she knew no amount of soap and water would make her feel less unclean. "I came here to suggest that you turn over whatever you have to Lee Michaels."

His bulbous eyes fixed on her. "Now why would you want to tell me to do that?"

"Because he'll be fair. And in the long run it'll be best for everybody." *Except me*, she admitted to herself. *There won't be any best for me ever again. Not without Lee.* "Toby and I can't live with these letters hanging over us, never knowing if they might be made public. Waiting . . . isn't always very good for people."

"The publicity could get pretty unpleasant," he pointed out.

"So it'll be in the newspaper, maybe on the national news for a day or two. Then it will be finished," she said sturdily. "We can handle that."

"Cripes." He glared at her in indecision.

Caitlin stood up. "May I use your phone?"

He waved her toward an expensive machine. Usually she would have been amused by its opulence. Now she studied it briefly to interpret its mass of buttons and high-tech features, and punched in a number from memory.

"University switchboard? President Silverthorne's home, please."

The operator began what Caitlin knew would be a diplomatic explanation of why the president couldn't be disturbed on Sunday afternoon.

She interrupted. "This is not a crank call. My name is Caitlin Stewart. I work at TPU—check your call sheet—and this is an emergency. If you aren't allowed to put me through, then I'll hang up, you ring the president and give him this number to call back." She read the Mallorys' number into the receiver, and added with meticulous politeness, "Please tell him that if he doesn't return the call within ten minutes, I'm coming to his house and camping on the doorstep. Have you got that? Good. Ten minutes."

She hung up. Ed grunted.

After two minutes, he said, "Silverthorne's your boss. You think the operator'll repeat exactly what you said?"

"I hope so." Caitlin sounded, and felt, indifferent. Tall Pines didn't form the center of her universe anymore.

"You could get fired. Any employee who gave me an ultimatum like that'd be out on her can."

"I'm quitting anyway." She wasn't sure when she had come to that decision, but she knew she'd stick to it. Toby's future, at least for the time being, was at TPU. Hers wasn't. Even without Lee.

Another minute crawled by. The phone jingled.

Caitlin lifted it on the first ring. "Yes, President. I'm at Ed Mallory's. He has something to talk over with you."

Flushing, Ed took the receiver in a hamlike fist and said, "Hello. I've got some letters here...."

Turning her back to allow him the pretense of privacy, she gazed out of the big picture window to the square old house that looked as homelike as ever. She wondered if Toby would want to live in it while he went to college, or if she should just put it on the market.

Ed harrumphed. She glanced around to find that he'd finished the phone conversation. "Back in a minute," he mumbled to her.

When he returned, he had a sandwich in one hand and a slim packet of envelopes in the other. "Here. He said I could trust you with them." Reluctantly, he added, "Guess I can."

"Thank you." Caitlin accepted the letters without enthusiasm, and left.

When she reached her own driveway, she slipped open the first envelope. Without reading the contents, she saw enough to recognize Jim's handwriting.

Flame, still sleeping on the hood of the car, stretched herself awake and poked at the windshield with her nose when Caitlin started the engine. She obviously thought another little ride, minus the cat carrier, an excellent idea. Caitlin let her in and plunked her down on the passenger side. "And stay there," she ordered. "Don't try jumping on my head while I drive."

It was a short distance to the imposing residence that bordered the campus. No sign marred the leafless expanse of beautifully maintained lawn, but a visitor would have had to be very naive to mistake this for anything but the presidential mansion. Broad columns rose two stories high. White paint, washed and touched up at the beginning of each school year by squads of student workers, sparkled in the weak autumn sun.

President Silverthorne himself came to the door at her ring.

If he had had any question about whether or when she'd show up, superb manners kept him from revealing it. "Mrs. Stewart, you've come to keep an old man company on Sunday afternoon. Bless you. Come in, come in."

Caitlin followed him through a corridor lined by paintings of former presidents into a cozy den at the rear of the building.

"Drafty old hulk. Already freezing and it's barely October. You should see the heating bills. This is the best room in the house. How was the lake?"

Caitlin jumped. "How did you know about that?"

He chuckled. "I have my spies."

"Yes," she said sadly. "I've become one of them." With an arm that felt numb, she passed him the letters.

"Ah. The famous letters. Mr. Michaels, will you fix Mrs. Stewart a drink?"

She whirled as he stepped out from a shadowy corner into the lighted area near a padded bar. "What would you like, Caitlin?"

She would have liked to run as fast and as far as her legs could carry her. As a grown woman, she accepted that that option was closed to her, so she stood with her gaze riveted on Lee.

He looked tired. His eyes were sunk deep in their sockets, which paradoxically had the effect of making them a more brilliant blue. Lines ran down his cheeks that hadn't been there yesterday. He'd shaved badly, so that here and there a dark whisker showed. She would have thought him dissipated if she hadn't known him.

His quick glance must have taken in the too-bright hazel eyes, as well as the red patch on each cheekbone she could see reflected in the mirror behind the bar, but he said only, "White wine?"

She achieved a tiny nod. Her fingers jerked and grazed the back of his hand as he passed her the glass.

It tilted. Caitlin righted it, trying not to show how close the fleeting contact brought her to tears.

"Don't worry," Lee said softly. She started. "It's not the same wine they serve at faculty parties," he added.

She couldn't smile. Nor could she drink. Not with Lee's steady, speculative gaze on her face.

"Top mine up, will you, my boy?" Silverthorne asked absently, holding out his tumbler as he skimmed through the sheaf of paper. Then he sipped thoughtfully and addressed Caitlin. "And what is it you wish us to do with these?"

"Whatever you think best."

"I see. You are here, then, as a member of the varsity Oversight Committee?"

Caitlin sighed. She'd operated all day on too little sleep. "Hardly. I'll be happy to give up my seat on the committee right now. As a matter of fact, I'm resigning from the library, too."

He shook out a huge square of linen and polished his trifocals. "Please don't put me to the trouble of refusing to accept. This seems to be a day for resignations. Mr. Michaels here was just informing me he's quitting the investigation when we got your—er—interesting message."

"Lee—" She looked at him wildly, then turned back to Silverthorne. Dealing with Lee was more than she could handle just now. "I'd hate to cause the university any more notoriety. There's been enough of that."

"We're in agreement there. However," he said with exaggerated kindness, as if explaining the facts of life to a dimwit, "your continued employment isn't germane to the issue at all. You're really quite irrelevant to the controversy. It would be more apt to inspire adverse comment if I did allow you to leave over this."

Caitlin wasn't sure if she should feel reassured or insulted, but she let the president take her by the hand. "Let me put it another way," she said. "I don't feel at home anymore at Tall Pines. I'll be leaving with or without your consent. Naturally, I'd rather have you agree because I don't want to break our contract. We both know you won't have any trouble finding a replacement."

"My dear, are you sure?" Silverthorne probed. Lee said nothing.

"It's the *only* thing I'm positive about," she replied frankly.

"Then you'll be needing recommendations," he said. "Are you going to broaden out from reference work? I can have my secretary contact . . ."

As Silverthorne outlined a plan of action, Lee picked up the discarded letters and began reading. The rustle of paper, his quiet breathing, interested Caitlin more than the president's excellent career advice.

Finally Lee dropped the letters into his lap. She gave up counterfeiting attention to Silverthorne's sonorous voice. Her head whipped around so swiftly a lock of red hair stung her cheek.

"Phone call," Lee said tersely, ignoring the perfectly good telephone that sat on the bar.

"Down the hall and to your right," said Silverthorne. "I presume you've changed your mind?" At Lee's blank, impatient look, he added, "About quitting the investigation."

"No point to it now. This stuff wraps it up. I'll see if I can talk my boss around to the position we already discussed." Wearily he added, "Caitie, I'm sorry. Damn it all, I really hoped it wouldn't come to this."

This time she was able to force a smile. "Go do your job, Lee."

He hesitated, nodded and left with that ground-eating stride that never even betrayed a limp. Given time and care, cells regenerated and molecules bonded. Tissue healed. She didn't feel any such confidence about the kinds of hurts she'd dealt herself since she'd met Lee, but her overwhelming need right now was privacy in which to lick her wounds in peace.

A few things remained that she had to know. The least important—least important to anyone but her—popped into her brain.

"Why was I put on the Oversight Committee?"

Amazingly, Silverthorne looked disconcerted.

"Not—not because you thought Lee Michaels and I—"

He changed the subject firmly. "As I was saying, you might want to consider moving into administration. Your organizational talents haven't been utilized behind the reference desk."

"Thank you. That's already occurred to me." Just as firmly, she turned the conversation back in the direction she wanted it to go. Silverthorne's kindness warmed her, but she was ready to plot her own course. "What should Toby and I expect from the media?"

Silverthorne grimaced. "I can tell you from Mr. Michaels that the conference isn't interested in blackening the reputation of a dead man. A statement will have to be issued, of course. We'll keep it low-key. The press is a different kettle of fish, while as for television... You're going to have to be prepared for the worst. The only good news, I'm afraid, is that these scandals come and go so quickly there will be another one to take its place in a month. Or a week."

The seconds ticking away scraped at Caitlin's nerves. Surely Lee would finish his phone call soon. The desire to spare both of them further embarrassment made her rush her farewell to Silverthorne.

She drove home at a reckless speed, braking twice to unwind Flame from the clutch. The drive used up the last of her energy. She parked and was sitting with her hands limp on the wheel when Flame gave an inquiring chirp and butted her thigh with a determined head.

"Want out, baby?" Caitlin asked. "Here you go."

The cat flowed to the ground and slunk away on her own pursuits. Caitlin moved unwarily and winced. Lee's lovemaking had called upon muscles unaccustomed to use. Combined with her emotional fatigue, the physical soreness was all the more noticeable. Worse than the pain, however, were the embers of desire it stirred. Every minuscule ache was exquisite because it reminded her of those hours in Lee's arms.

Dwelling on the memory was pointless, she told herself. Her misjudgment of him was too grievous for her to expect, or deserve, forgiveness. The only thing to do was to keep out of his way. And hope for his sake he found it easier to forget her than she would to forget him.

Restless, she wandered into the living room and studied the picture of Jim she'd taken so long ago. It looked the same as ever—a portrait of the heroic football coach, sun-washed, wind-lashed, his character caught and preserved forever in a photograph.

How much had been Jim, and how much the loving eye of the photographer? Had she ever known the real man at all?

A sense of déjà vu gripped her as the doorbell chimed. This had happened before. She'd stood in this spot, the bell had rung and . . .

"I'll get it," yelled Toby.

At the familiar male rumble, butterflies came alive in Caitlin's abdomen. She froze.

Toby and Lee spoke quietly. Only the lowest vibrations penetrated the walls, but she had no difficulty separating Toby's lighter tones from the kettledrum of Lee's bass. *I can hear his voice in my bones*, she thought.

Exerting more discipline than she'd believed she possessed, Caitlin stayed still until she heard the screen door slam shut and Toby came into the room.

"Here," he said. He held out her overnight bag. "The other stuff is in the hall. Lee said to give you this, too. And here's the mail from yesterday. It was in the box."

She didn't know what she expected in the envelope from Lee. A note, perhaps, containing recriminations for running away, first from the hotel and then from the president's mansion. What she found was Lee's personal check, made out to C. Stewart, for the exact amount she'd paid at the hotel. In another envelope, postmarked Seattle, was an invitation from the football conference office to interview for the head archivist's job.

"So looking forward . . ." she read.

Something crashed on the porch.

Toby barely beat her into the hall. She got there in time to see Lee lift his foot and kick the frame of the screen again.

Caitlin's supercharged nerves found relief in screaming. "What the devil do you think you're doing, Lee Michaels?"

"Trying to get your attention," he said, holding up his hands to display Flame doing her best to escape his grasp.

Caitlin rubbed her temples.

"I was going out to sit in my car and plan my next method of approach. You didn't think I was quietly fading out of your life, did you? Innocent Cait. At any rate, there she was, sharpening her claws on my leather upholstery. She took exception when I asked her—very politely, I assure you—to cut it out. Brute force was necessary."

"Oh, hell," muttered Caitlin. She shoved open the screen. Lee dropped on one knee to release Flame, who put her pink nose in the air and stalked off.

Toby edged backward toward the kitchen. "Excuse me. I'll just—uh—excuse me."

Caitlin looked sullen. She felt sullen. The nobility of her silent pledge to avoid Lee had been wasted. He was here in his all-too-glorious flesh.

Lee had dreaded this moment every inch of the way from the president's house. But seeing Caitlin glower, he suddenly felt rather cheerful. Sulks were easier to deal with than rage.

"She didn't scratch you," Caitlin offered finally.

"No, I remembered the last time. I waited until her back was turned and grabbed the scruff of her neck in one hand and her rump in the other. It didn't immobilize her, but it did cut down on her offensive capability."

"Thank you for bringing her in. And, um, thanks for this," said Caitlin, handing him the check, "but I can't possibly accept it."

"May I ask why not?"

"It does rather smack of payment for services rendered, don't you think?"

He proffered it again between index and middle finger. Caitlin put her hands behind her back.

Lee tossed the check onto the hall table. "Look, I'll admit to being a reactionary. I am the man. You are the woman. We went somewhere together and I consider it my responsibility to pay. Be gracious and take the damned money!"

His amusement goaded Caitlin beyond endurance. She picked up the check and tore it in half.

"For a bright woman, you do the stupidest things," he said as if he were strangling.

"Then just be glad you've been saved from your lapse into bad taste!" she shot back.

"Since when is it bad taste for a man to pay for a date?"

Caitlin could feel heat scorch her face. "I meant bad taste in being attracted to me."

"Oh, but I always go for stupid women. The stupider the better," Lee said encouragingly.

Caitlin snapped, "Well, you've got them standing in line. Tamara—"

"Who? Oh, her."

"That ditzy secretary at school, the salesclerk at the jewelry store—"

Lee was smiling. Caitlin swallowed.

"Anyway," she said, "going to a hotel isn't a date. It's an encounter."

"No," he said positively. "What we did was making love, Cait. Love."

She couldn't sustain the force of his gaze. His eyes were the blue of lake water reflecting the sky and filled with light. She looked away.

"Besides, if you won't let me reimburse you, you've as good as paid me for yesterday. That hurts my feelings. You know I'm sensitive about being a sex object."

Caitlin sucked her lips between her teeth. "I suppose the next thing for me to do," he added, "is call the hotel and have them adjust the balance on your charge card. I'll have to use mine to do it, but I sort of like the idea of our credit cards tangled in some inextricable fiscal embrace—"

"You can't!"

He sighed. "What did you use, the gold fillings in your teeth?"

"If it's any of your business, Lee Michaels, and it's not, I did pay with plastic. I'm not dependent on you."

"I'm glad to hear it. A woman of property. I *do* have good taste." He continued thoughtfully, "I suppose I could get Toby to sneak the money into your savings account."

"If you dare—"

"Or, I know, I'll ask Auretta to steal a deposit slip from your purse. She'll do it. Auretta likes me."

A stifled giggle broke from Caitlin. "Stop that! You're making me laugh on purpose!"

"I told you once I'm not a nice guy around you. Cat eyes bring out the beast in me."

He took a step toward her, but she fended him off with a whispered "Don't!" Her eyes seemed to have grown to fill a third of her face. The pupils were big and black with distress.

"Lee, we can't go on from here and pretend how I behaved doesn't matter!"

He smiled wryly. "It was daunting, I have to admit, when you didn't come back to our room. I assumed you were someplace on the grounds walking off your anger. There's nothing to be ashamed of if you went a little crazy for a while. I didn't mean to be so clumsy telling you about—"

"Jim," she finished for him. "Don't be ridiculous. You were the soul of tact and honor. I'm the one who denounced you in front of about forty strangers, fled in the night in a laundry truck—"

"Did you? Oh, poor Cait." Lee's shoulders were shaking. "Did Toby tell you I'm not very popular with Brenda's parents anymore?"

Caitlin glared at him. "Yes, he did. And I didn't ride in the truck the whole way."

He was so much everything a woman could want that she felt her heart breaking all over again. She said, "Being in love isn't a great aid to clear thinking. I knew my judgment was nonexistent where you were concerned, so when you told me about Jim, I couldn't trust myself to believe you. I chose a lie instead of the truth."

Without seeming to move, Lee closed the distance between them. He ran a hand over her hair and down her cheek. His touch was incendiary. Caitlin gasped as if burned.

"Dear heart, nobody could blame you for reacting the way you did. Having your idol knocked down is bound to cause some trauma. The fact is—listen to me—Jim was a fine man. He had a blind spot about his work, that's all."

She shivered. "Are you thinking I could condemn him? My faults are much worse. I was married to somebody I never got to know very well. It wasn't a marriage at all, just sharing sex and a house. And I called it love."

"Stop beating yourself, Cait."

He was caressing the soft area under her chin with one thumb. Caitlin jerked her head away.

"I don't want to be forgiven for the rest of my life!"

Lee looked pleased. "I'm glad. It sounds exhausting. I'll tell you what. Since we evidently need to learn more about each other, we can hop over to the county clerk's office on your lunch break tomorrow and see about the license. Then we'll have the next three days to further our acquaintance before the wedding."

He halted Caitlin's sputtering sounds with his thumb. "Don't you know it's rude to interrupt? The best part is, after that we can take the rest of our lives to get to know each other really well. Doesn't that make sense?"

His voice and touch were working like a drug on Caitlin's resistance. She forced herself to murmur against his thumb, "I can tell how you want to know me, and it's in the biblical sense."

"That's true," he agreed. "Caitie Cat Eyes, you turn my bones to water. But I—how can I prove to you we need each other body and soul?"

Her body was already convinced. Lee's free arm gathered her close. His proximity was so demoralizing that the effort not to stand on tiptoe and rub herself against his taut, solid hips produced a fine prickling of sweat under her clothes. Her mind clung to its qualms.

"If you loved me, you'd hate me," she blurted.

She was so adorable, he thought. And so maddening.

"I'll work on it," he promised. "Right now I'm about at the end of my patience. Will you or will you not marry me?"

She had to lean her head way back to see his face. His classic mouth was stern and his eyelids crinkled with determination, hinting at how he would look after forty or fifty more years of living. She would never tire of waking to his face.

And the man within? Apparently she wasn't a good judge of men. She'd never looked closely enough to notice Jim's feet of clay. But Lee was here, now, and as near perfection as she could imagine a husband to be. But even if the coming years revealed a flaw or two masked by her own love for him, she knew disappointment wouldn't change her feelings. Loving Lee was as natural to her as breathing.

If she said no today, she thought, she really would lose him forever.

"I don't understand why you're here," she said. At his look of astonishment, she added, "I mean, I accept that you love me. I just don't understand how you could."

He pressed his hands into her shoulders. They felt heavy, intimate, impossible to ignore.

"The list is a mile long. You're smart and pretty. Good company. We think alike, and our emotions run in the same direction. And remember, I told you about the friend who banged up my knee? I couldn't bear to lose you to guilt, too."

Her haunted eyes locked onto his. His chin jutted. "But you want the reason behind all the other reasons, right? And the answer is, I don't know." He shrugged. "I couldn't meet you and not love you. Simple as that."

He decided this was too slow. Maybe he needed to fall back on the lesson Caitlin herself had taught him at her lake cabin. Words alone couldn't penetrate the complicated maze of her emotions. The time for subtlety had passed.

Deliberately, he put forefinger and thumb to one of her breasts where the nubbin already pushed against her T-shirt. He drew the tight button of flesh between his fingers over and over. Her mouth went soft and willing. He bent to it but not for a kiss. His tongue lashed straight for hers.

His other hand—not the one sweetly torturing her breast—literally scooped her up to fit her into the bowl of his hips. Caitlin wriggled to escape, but that was a mistake. Sharp pleasure burst out in precise little flashes at every movement. She tried to stay still, but his iron hand, jammed against her bottom, and the other hardness, a hot promise against her thighs, wouldn't let her.

His hands demanded; the deep, calming voice gentled. "That's right, Caitie. Don't stop, honey. Show me how you love me."

His approval thrust her farther into the maelstrom of sensation.

"The way we feel about each other is not just sex."

"No," she agreed, tears and laughter coming together. Lee was right. She did love him. Her body knew it, he knew it, she knew it.

"Although the sex isn't bad."

"The sex is *wonderful*," she contradicted. Putting her arms around his neck, she stroked the rigid muscles at his nape.

Very slowly, so she couldn't help but be aware of every contour of his taut loins and hips, he let her slide to her feet. "Okay, those are points one and two. We love each other, we're good together—and not just in bed. We care about the same sorts of things. Honesty and integrity and work that matters. You and I want the same life, with kids and the time to enjoy them. Oh, God, Caitie, don't cry. Please. I swore I wouldn't ravish you unless you wanted it. I shouldn't have joked. But I thought if I made you feel the way you love me—I know you love me, Caitlin."

She scrubbed tears from her cheeks. "Elizabeth Barrett Browning couldn't count all the ways I love you."

"Then we can work through anything else."

She closed her eyes to shut out the distracting sight of love and fear in his face.

Lee said for the last time, "Will you marry me?"

Caitlin opened her eyes. "Are you sure we have to wait four days?"

He cupped her face in his hands. "Not for everything—that is, if you still want—"

"I want. I definitely want."

He picked her up and started for the stairs. "Where's Toby?"

"Doesn't matter. He's got his own girl," Caitlin said. At the top of the stairs, her voice light and urgent, she directed, "My room."

He maneuvered them both through the door and placed her on her feet. The yearning to feel Lee within her was fast building to an overmastering need. She tore off her T-shirt and began clawing clumsily at the snap of her jeans.

Lee said, "All right, you, beat it."

"What?" she gasped, and turned to see Lee carefully shoveling the slumbering Flame off the quilt. He stood for a moment, then simply shoved the limp feline under the bed.

He was naked already. Caitlin forgot to move.

"Is it all right if I tell you how beautiful you are?" she asked.

"Just this once." A grin transformed the finely etched lines of his mouth. "Maybe I could grow a hunchback. Or get my nose broken."

"Oh, don't do it just for me," Caitlin told him. "But if you did, I'd still love the person behind your eyes."

As she struggled with the closure of her pants, her small, round breasts swayed slightly. Lee thought they were lush and perfect.

"Caitlin, don't you know you're the beautiful one? Here, I will," he said, and deftly set to work on the snap.

"You're a brave man."

"Am I?"

"Considering what my cat keeps trying to do to you . . ." Caitlin touched the black pelt covering Lee's chest with a delicate finger. The hairs sprang back. "Your scratches are almost healed. I forgot to look before."

"You have to know how to handle golden-eyed redheads. Oh, wait a minute." He retrieved something from his pants pocket and slid it back on her finger. The ring.

Caitlin admired it while he returned to the job at hand. Her jeans were a tight fit. He tugged and she said, "Ouch!"

"Cait, what is it? Did I hurt you?"

She smiled up at him. "No, just a reminder from yesterday."

"I hurt you then? Honey, why didn't you say so? Maybe we shouldn't—"

Caitlin stepped out of her jeans. "Lee, until you showed up I hadn't had a date in three years, let alone a lover. Muscles need to be exercised."

She reached out boldly. He tensed at her touch. What she was doing to him had its effect on her, too. Her breath began to come in soft gasps and her body crowded closer to his. For a few frantic, amazingly exciting minutes, her hands could be everywhere, savoring. Then Lee removed the piece of nylon that still separated them and they were on the bed, mouths supplicating in a kiss that was even more exciting.

The raw need she tasted on his lips and tongue overcame any lingering constraints of time or place. Her heart thumped frantically at the thought that *Lee* sprawled across her bed, sliding a leg between hers, teasing her breasts until he reawoke the tiny, hot pulses of pleasure he'd roused in her downstairs.

The double bed had never seemed small before, but he dwarfed it. A chance glimpse of Lee's feet, stretching beyond the mattress by a number of inches, made her chuckle shakily. They would need a larger bed when they moved to Seattle.

"What is it?" His dark-lashed lids were heavy with sensual concentration, but his grin, though faint, remained reassuringly crooked. "Please don't tell me something's wrong."

"Nothing's wrong," she said. "Everything's right. Do you like it when I do this?" Her tongue sought sensitive flesh.

His breath caught. "*Like* might be understating how . . . Honey, you're going to drive me to reciprocate."

After he reciprocated, making her writhe and bury her fingers in his thick black hair, he pulled away to pile pillows against the headboard.

"Love," she whispered, "when we have our first anniversary, there's a special way I'd like to celebrate."

"Anything. Tell me."

"With a three-month birthday party for our baby."

He sat up and opened his arms.

Taking him inside her, she folded him as tight and close as she could. His eyes had little blue flames in them that held her hypnotized even after he eased her forward and dipped his head to her breasts. The pleasure in loving, in mating, grew too intense to hang on to. She felt tossed so high that Lee alone held her earthbound. Satisfaction burst within her and she cried out, again and again, as his hoarse shout echoed in the quiet room.

Drifting back to the present, Caitlin became aware of an intrusive paw patting her toes. Flame had woken up.

"What a pest," she said fondly. "Scat!"

Lee ran his palms up and down her arms, as if the desire she roused in him could be temporarily quenched but never extinguished. "Don't make her go on my account."

Caitlin looked at him doubtfully. "Sure? She's been awfully mean to you."

He smiled into her golden eyes. "That's all right," he said. "I like cats."

HARLEQUIN Temptation

COMING NEXT MONTH

In April, Harlequin brings you the world's most popular romance author

JANET DAILEY

No Quarter Asked

Out of print since 1974!

After the tragic death of her father, Stacy's world is shattered. She needs to get away by herself to sort things out. She leaves behind her boyfriend, Carter Price, who wants to marry her. However, as soon as she arrives at her rented cabin in Texas, Cord Harris, owner of a large ranch, seems determined to get her to leave. When Stacy has a fall and is injured, Cord reluctantly takes her to his own ranch. Unknown to Stacy, Carter's father has written to Cord and asked him to keep an eye on Stacy and try to convince her to return home. After a few weeks there, in spite of Cord's hateful treatment that involves her working as a ranch hand and the return of Lydia, his ex-fiancée, by the time Carter comes to escort her back, Stacy knows that she is in love with Cord and doesn't want to go.

**Watch for *Fiesta San Antonio* in July and
For Bitter or Worse in September.**

JDA-1

Have You Ever Wondered If You Could Write A Harlequin Novel?

Here's great news—Harlequin is offering a series of cassette tapes to help you do just that. Written by Harlequin editors, these tapes give practical advice on how to make your characters—and your story— come alive. There's a tape for each contemporary romance series Harlequin publishes.

Mail order only

All sales final

This April, don't miss Harlequin's new Award of
Excellence title from

Harlequin Presents...

CAROLE MORTIMER

Award of Excellence

---

elusive as the unicorn

*When Eve Eden discovered that Adam
Gardener, successful art entrepreneur, was
searching for the legendary English artist, The
Unicorn, she nervously shied away. The Unicorn's
true identity hit too close to home....*

*Besides, Eve was rattled by Adam's
mesmerizing presence, especially in the light
of the ridiculous coincidence of their names—
and his determination to take advantage of it!
But Eve was already engaged to marry her
longtime friend, Paul.*

*Yet Eve found herself troubled by the different
choices Adam and Paul presented. If only the
answer to her dilemma didn't keep eluding her....*

HP1258-1

HARLEQUIN Temptation

The Adventurer

JAYNE ANN KRENTZ

Remember THE PIRATE (Temptation #287), the first book of Jayne Ann Krentz's exciting trilogy Ladies and Legends? Next month Jayne brings us another powerful romance, THE ADVENTURER (Temptation #293), in which Kate, Sarah and Margaret — three long-time friends featured in THE PIRATE — meet again.

A contemporary version of a great romantic myth, THE ADVENTURER tells of Sarah Fleetwood's search for long-lost treasure and for love. Only when she meets her modern-day knight-errant Gideon Trace will Sarah know she's found the path to fortune and eternal bliss....

THE ADVENTURER — available in April 1990! And in June, look for THE COWBOY (Temptation #302), the third book of this enthralling trilogy.

T293-1